ALIENS, GHOSTS, AND VANISHINGS

For Peter,
for everything

A Random House book
Published by Penguin Random House Australia
Level 3, 100 Pacific Highway, North Sydney NSW 2060
www.penguin.com.au

Penguin
Random House
Australia

First published by Random House Australia in 2016

Text copyright © Stella Tarakson 2016
Illustrations copyright © Richard Morden 2016

Addresses for the Penguin Random House group of companies can be found at global.penguinrandomhouse.com/offices.

National Library of Australia
Cataloguing-in-Publication Entry

Author: Tarakson, Stella
Title: Aliens, Ghosts and Vanishings
ISBN: 978 1 92532 496 9 (hardback)
Target Audience: For children
Subjects: Children's questions and answers
          Australia – Miscellanea – Juvenile literature
Other Creators/Contributors: Morden, Richard, illustrator
Dewey Number: 994

Cover design by Christa Moffitt, Christabella Designs
Cover and internal illustrations by Richard Morden
Internal design and typesetting by Midland Typesetters,
based on original design by Christa Moffitt, Christabella Designs
Printed and bound in China by RR Donnelley

ALIENS, GHOSTS, AND VANISHINGS

STRANGE AND POSSIBLY TRUE AUSTRALIAN STORIES

STELLA TARAKSON

ILLUSTRATED BY RICHARD MORDEN

RANDOM HOUSE AUSTRALIA

CONTENTS

TREADING THE PATH:
TO BELIEVE OR NOT TO BELIEVE?

You may have heard of the Loch Ness monster, the *Mary Celeste* ghost ship and the mysterious disappearances in the Bermuda Triangle. Can this bizarre creature, this mysterious ship, and these worrying vanishings be explained by science or do they defy logic? Nobody knows for sure, but one thing is certain: they have all inspired world-famous tales and sparked fierce curiosity and debate.

Did you know that Australia has its own share of amazing myths and mysteries? It shouldn't be surprising, given the size of this huge country. Some of the myths and mysteries in this book may be familiar to you. You might have heard tales of

bunyips and yowies, and whispers of hauntings and mysterious disappearances. But how much do we really know about the incredible things that happen on our own doorstep? For instance, have you heard about the falling stones at Mayanup? Or the UFO sightings on the Nullarbor Plain? And what about the ancient Egyptian hieroglyphs found not far from Sydney?

Of course, you can't believe everything you hear. The best approach to the information you'll encounter in these pages is to keep an open mind. Ferret out the facts, ruminate on the rumours, and analyse alternative explanations. Perhaps even ask

yourself why people might make such claims in the first place. Do they have something to gain? Are they honestly mistaken? Or are they telling the plain unvarnished truth?

Everyone has their own way of judging information. Gullibility, or believing without question, is one extreme. The other is absolute scepticism, where a mind is so firmly shut that no new thoughts can enter. Both extremes have their dangers and the best path to tread is somewhere in the middle. But be warned: that path can be hard to find. It twists and turns. And sometimes it gets lost in the shadows . . .

MYTHICAL CREATURES

Zoology is the scientific study of animals, their behaviour, diet and habitat. Zoologists are interested in how animals evolve over time, how they interact with each other and how they fit into their environment. They don't, however, study animals that might not be real – bizarre creatures that lurk on the fringes of existence, hidden from sight. That's the domain of cryptozoologists.

Cryptozoology literally means the study of hidden animals – 'crypto' comes from the Greek word *kryptos*, which means 'hidden'. Cryptozoologists investigate cryptids, animals that are only rumoured to exist, such as Scotland's Loch Ness monster. Cryptozoology is mainly based on reports of sightings. There is rarely any physical evidence that can be tested, such as animal droppings, hairs or skeletons. As there is so little to study, it is not considered a true branch of science.

Mind you, it has led to some amazing discoveries. Ever heard of the kraken? Said to live off the coast of Norway and Greenland, this gigantic sea monster was once blamed for shipwrecks. According to legend, the kraken would wrap its many tentacles around a ship, capsize it and pull it under the waves. It sounds fanciful, but there's a real animal that comes close to matching the kraken's description. It's called the colossal squid. Although not as big and fearsome as stories imply the legendary kraken is, the colossal squid is a known aquatic species. It may well be that sightings of the colossal squid led to the creation of the kraken myth in the first place.

Who knows how many new animals are waiting to be found, perhaps by cryptozoologists here in Australia?

There's certainly no shortage of mysterious creatures being reported across the country. It might be a good idea to invest in a pair of binoculars, just in case you come across one . . .

This mythical creature has some basis in reality. Although the existence of kraken hasn't yet been proved, there are certainly gigantic squids.

BUNYiPS

Bunyips are known for their gleaming eyes and bloodcurdling screams. Lurking in swamps, billabongs and other water-holes, they're mostly active at night. This makes them hard to see, but when they have been spotted, they've typically been described as looking like a cross between a mammal, a reptile and a bird. Are these scary swamp monsters real or just legends?

Indigenous origins

Long before the British arrived, Indigenous Australians spoke of encounters with monsters that lurked in billabongs and water-holes. Large, man-eating creatures with bellowing voices and glinting eyes. But what did they look like? The swamp monsters have been described as being either fish-like, mammal-like, or bird-like, with either scales, fur or feathers. Some are said to be combinations of all three. But this mix-up isn't too surprising. Glimpses of the beast have been only fleeting. After all, if you were confronted by a bloodthirsty bunyip and feared for your life, would you sit around taking notes?

Today there are numerous Indigenous family groups scattered throughout Australia, and before 1788 there were many, many more. In his book *Bunyips: Australia's Folklore of Fear*, Robert Holden explains that while many family groups and regions had longstanding stories of swamp monsters, the descriptions of these monsters varied markedly. To make things even more confusing, there were hundreds of Indigenous languages and dialects. There were so many different names for the swamp beast, it's difficult to be certain that everyone was talking about the same thing. Even so, when the British came and heard the tales, they eventually settled on just one name – bunyip.

Information about bunyip sightings was originally passed down through generations of Indigenous Australian families, much of it in the oral tradition, through spoken stories and songs. Sometimes pictures of 'bunyips' were also drawn, to go with the story. Each storyteller added their own twist to the tale, yet the message remained the same. Beware the swamp monster. Beware the bunyip!

British colonists

Some early settlers befriended Indigenous people, who warned them about swamp monsters and the dangers of straying near waterholes at night. The colonists took these stories very seriously. They had to rely on the Indigenous people's knowledge and skills when it came to surviving in the harsh Australian conditions. And why would they doubt what they were being told? The animals the British encountered in Australia were unlike any they had ever seen before. In a strange land where kangaroos,

frill-necked lizards and platypuses were a reality, almost anything could be true!

The first recorded sighting of a bunyip by a British person was connected to William Buckley, an escaped convict. His experiences are described in Tim Flannery's book *The Life and Adventures of William Buckley*. Known as the 'wild white man', Buckley lived with an Indigenous family group for over 30 years in the early 1800s. When Buckley eventually returned to town, he described his encounter with a bunyip. Buckley had only ever seen the beast's back, which he said was covered with grey feathers. He said it was the size of a calf and only appeared when the weather was calm and the water was smooth.

Since then, many more people have claimed to have seen or heard bunyips in the bush. Most Australians today are familiar with the concept, even if we're not quite sure what the beasts are.

Bunyips in the Australian government!

The word 'bunyip' became a common Aussie slang term. In the mid-1800s, it was used to refer to an impostor or con man – that is, somebody pretending to be someone they're not. This hints that most people had stopped seriously believing in bunyips by then. The slang term slowly fell out of use. However, in the 1990s, Prime Minister Paul Keating, who had quite a way with words, famously used the word 'bunyip' to describe the opposition party. By that, he meant the politicians couldn't be trusted and their promises should not be believed.

What could they be?

Descriptions of bunyips vary, but one thing that stays the same across most accounts is the booming, screeching sound they make. This could in fact refer to any number of real creatures. Possums can be surprisingly loud, as can certain birds, such as barking owls and bitterns.

But what if sightings of bunyips aren't just due to people mistaking real animals? What if the bunyip really did once exist? Some researchers think the bunyip legend originated in eyewitness accounts of real animals tens of thousands of years ago. Stories of the sightings were passed down among Indigenous people, with details morphing and changing after countless generations of telling and retelling.

These researchers point to the diprotodon in particular. Diprotodons were once part of Australia's megafauna – unusually large animals that died out thousands of years ago. The diprotodon was a four-legged marsupial. It was a herbivore, which means that it only ate plants, but even so, the powerfully built animal would have been a fearsome sight because it was taller than a human being! The diprotodon became extinct a long time ago. Scientists don't agree on when this actually happened. Some think the animals became extinct around 50,000 years ago, while others believe it was closer to 25,000 years. Either way, Indigenous Australians have been here long enough to have lived with diprotodons for thousands of years.

In the book *Kadimakara: Extinct Vertebrates of Australia,* authors Dr Pat Vickers-Rich and Gerard van Tets note that some Indigenous people, when shown the bones of a diprotodon, identified them as belonging to a bunyip. It's a reasonable solution to the origins of the legend – ancient memories being passed down the generations. However, that doesn't explain why the sightings continue to this day. After all, bones don't scream in the night!

The Australian Museum's bunyip display

Established in 1827, the Australian Museum in Sydney is our oldest museum. Known for its extensive range of animal specimens and fossils, it also carries out world-class scientific research. Right from the start, the museum's aim was to obtain 'many rare and curious specimens of Natural History'. A worthy goal, but it once resulted in a rather dubious display.

In 1846, the museum exhibited a purported bunyip skull. Retrieved from the banks of the Murrumbidgee River, the skull was thought to belong to an unknown species. It was considered a scientific breakthrough and it drew a great deal of excited attention. However, an expert soon declared it was actually the deformed skull of an unborn foal or calf. The 'bunyip' skull was only on display for two days before it was sheepishly removed.

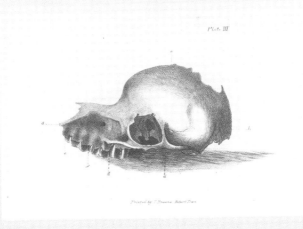

Illustration of the 'bunyip' skull, reproduced from
The Tasmanian Journal of Natural Science, January 1849.

YOWIES

Known as Australia's Big Foot, is this shy ape-like beast just a legend, or an undiscovered human species?

A long history of sightings

The first reported sighting of a yowie came one year after the British colonisation of Australia. Back in 1789, a particularly hairy wild man was purportedly captured at Botany Bay. He was shipped back to England for study, arriving alive and well. According to the report, the man was nearly three metres tall and had huge teeth, thick eyebrows, and a body covered with strong black hair. His toenails and fingernails were like talons, and he was considered to be the largest man in the world at the time.

Does this sound too fanciful to be true? The report was titled: *A description of a wonderful large wild man, or monstrous giant, brought from Botany-Bay.* It's available on the New South Wales

A DESCRIPTION of a wonderful large WILD MAN, or monstrous GIANT, BROUGHT FROM BOTANY-BAY.

THERE has been many various Reports concerning this moſt ſurpriſing WILD MAN or huge ſavage GIANT, that was brought from *Botany-Bay to England*, numbers of People arguing and diſputing about his enormous Size, but to prevent further contending, the following is ſufficient to ſatisfy the Reader as many Thouſands have ſeen him in *Plymouth*, where he was landed alive and in good health. A Gentleman of this Country being lately in *Plymouth* was curious enough for he took a View of the GIANT, he being the firſt that ever was brought from *Botany-Bay* to this kingdom. --- therefore this Gentleman of veracity brought the printed Account of him, which gives a Deſcription of the wonderful Size, Form, Shape Features and Complexion of this aſtoniſhing GIANT : alſo an Account after the Manner that he was taken by a Crew of Engliſh Sailors, and brought over from *Batany-Bay*, and explained in the following Manner.

THIS ſurpriſing monſtrous Giant was taken by a crew of Engliſh Sailors when they went on ſhore to furniſh themſelves with freſh water at Botany-bay. To their ſurpriſe they beheld at a diſtance three of the moſt ſurpriſing talleſt and biggeſt looking naked men that have been ſeen in the memory of this age, turning towards them, which much affrighted the ſailors, cauſed them to make expedition on board the ſhip for the ſafety of their lives, leaving the caſks of water and a quantity of good old rum which they had in a cag to refreſh themſelves and make merry, when the three ſavages got to the ſea-ſide they ſtared at the ſhip for a long time with wonder and admiration, one of them having got the cag of rum, he taſted, ſpit it out and ſhook his head, another did the ſame, but the third drank plenſifully, and began to jump about in a frightful wild manner, ſhouting and makeing a hideous noiſe, the other two Giants went off and left this one enjoying the cag of rum, who drank to ſuch exceſs that he dropped on the ground and lay as if dead the ſailors went on ſhore well armed and found this monſtruous body motionleſs! they bound him faſt with ropes and with much fatigue got him on board the ſhip, where they ſecured him with iron chains, where he ſlept upwards of 24 hours before he was awake and was kept chained during the paſſage, he ſhewed not the leaſt token of ill-neſs at ſea, he came in the ſhip Rover, capt. Lee to England from Botany-Bay, and landed at Plymouth, November 29, 1789.

Ladies and gentlemen in great numbers honored him with their company, and has been ſeen by thouſands of people, and all acknowledge him to be the greateſt curioſity ever ſeen in England by the oldeſt man living, he being ſuch a monſtrous overgrown ſize and being the firſt ever brought from that country captain Lee determined to bring him to London: he is much

tamer, and not ſo ſavage in temper as might be expected. He is 9 feet 7 inches high, 4 feet 10 inches broad, a remarkable large head, broad face, frightful eyes, a broad noſe and thick lips like a black, very broad teeth, heavy eye-brows, hair ſtronger than a horſe's mane, a long beard ſtrong as black wire, body and limbs covered with ſtrong black hair, the nails of his fingers and toes may be properly called talons, crookt like a hawk's bill, and as hard as horn, in ſhort he is viewed with admiration and aſtoniſhment on account of his huge ſize.

He is allowed to be the greateſt curioſity in England, being the largeſt man in the known world, though ſome ſay there are larger in New Holland. He reſembles a black, but his ſkin is yellow. The ſailors who brought him over ſay when they took him he was curiouſly painted moſtly with red. There are red, green and blue mines where he came from, and delight in painting their ſkin. The captain ſays that before he got this wild ſavage into cuſtody he took a cloſe view of them with a ſpyinggalſs from the ſhip and of the other two giants that were with him which he thought were his ſons, for they looked young and had little or no beard, and had variety of red circles and ſpot and ſtripes on their bodies and limbs which they ſeemed to admire. This giant is very wild and knows nothing of chriſtianity he has offered to ſhew many acts of violence, but is fond of his keeper, and is more calm in his temper. He is chained round the middle, but has liberty to lie down, and riſe and ſit, and walks ſome yards when he chuſes. They take great pains to inſtruct him in the Engliſh tongue, and it is hoped in time he will be made to talk and become a chriſtian. He will ſometimes go willingly, eat human fleſh if he can get it, but now ſeems to alter his mind: he was a long time muzzled.—This is a full deſcription.

Excerpt from the 1789 report, describing a 'wonderful large wild man', later known as a yowie.

State Library's manuscripts, oral history and pictures website, so you can see it for yourself! See 'Want more?' on page 44.

Mind you, the wild man wasn't called a yowie back then. Rather, he was described as a 'most surprising wild man or huge savage giant'. It was said he would eat human flesh if he could get it, but was fond of his keeper. Not in an eating way, that is. Attempts were even made to teach the wild man to speak English!

It didn't take long for supposedly Indigenous stories of hairy giants to spread throughout the colony. The beasts were called yowies or sometimes yahoos, and hundreds of sightings followed, all matching those of the unfortunate wild man. Most witnesses also reported a pungent odour attached to the creature, as well as a guttural growling beyond the human vocal range. Reports continue into the present day. Most sightings have occurred at night and in remote areas. Unlike bunyips, however, descriptions of yowies have remained remarkably consistent. Does this mean they are more likely to be true?

Overseas relatives

Do yowies sound familiar? They share startling similarities with the apelike cryptids of other countries. You've probably heard of the sasquatch, also known as Big Foot, said to inhabit dense forests in the United States and Canada. And there's the yeti, also known as the abominable snowman, which supposedly lurks in the Himalaya Mountains. The yeti is often reported as having white hair rather than black – to blend in with the snow perhaps – but otherwise it is described much like a yowie. And like yowies, sightings of Big Foot and yetis go back hundreds of years. There have been literally thousands of sightings. Can they all be wrong?

Is the Australian yowie related to America's Big Foot or the Himalayan yeti?

A need for evidence

First we need to ask whether there is any hard evidence that the yowie exists. Although modern technology means that anyone with a computer and too much free time can produce convincing images, it doesn't mean that everyone is lying. Some purported sightings might just be honest mistakes, where glimpses of known animals are misconstrued. As for the others . . . Is it possible that some are genuine?

What's needed is physical proof. Over the years, several people have claimed to have captured Big Foot. Each time, these claims have turned out to be a hoax. In 2014, the Royal Society of London, known for world-class scientific research, published the results of genetic tests on hair samples attributed to Big Foot and the yeti. The results found that most of the samples belonged to known animals including bears, dogs, horses and even humans. Some results were more puzzling, but still didn't point to a new species. One sample, for example, ended up matching DNA recovered from the fossil of an extinct animal. Another was thought to contain hairs from a previously unknown type of bear.

Even so, cryptozoologists haven't been discouraged. They point to footprints that appear to have been left by the gigantic cryptids. Casts have been taken of these huge footprints – some in dirt, some embedded in rock – which are far too big to have been made by humans. Some have been exposed as hoaxes, but many others aren't so clear cut. Could they provide that elusive evidence of an unknown species of man or animal?

For more information and to help you judge for yourself, visit Dean Harrison's Australian Yowie Research website (see 'Want more?' on page 44). It contains information on sightings, photographs, and witness sketches. Balancing an open mind with a healthy degree of scepticism is recommended!

A link in the chain of evolution?

Some researchers speculate that yowies, Big Foot and yetis are surviving examples of Gigantopithecus, an extinct giant ape. Palaeontologists don't know for sure, however, whether these apes walked upright or on all fours. Furthermore, fossils of these creatures have only ever been found in Asia. It's unlikely that Gigantopithecus migrated to all the places where the wild hairy human-like beasts have been spotted. This has led others to wonder whether yowies could actually be an unknown species of hominin: an extinct (or nearly extinct!) human species. Perhaps an unknown branch of our family tree?

The Royal Society report pointed out that absence of evidence is not evidence of absence. Just because you can't prove something exists, that doesn't mean it doesn't!

Palaeontology versus cryptozoology

Palaeontologists are scientists who study fossils. The word *palaeo* is the Greek word for 'old'. Here we're talking very, very old. Palaeontologists are looking for evidence of animals that are long extinct, such as dinosaurs. They also try to trace human evolution back into the mists of time.

Palaeontology is different from cryptozoology because cryptozoologists seek evidence of animals that they believe are *currently* alive. Palaeontologists and cryptozoologists share many of the same difficulties, however. Finding evidence of something that roamed the earth many millions of years ago isn't easy. Remains are few and far between, and isolated fossils can sometimes be interpreted in more than one way. Mistakes have been made on several occasions, and learning from these errors is one way in which the science progresses.

Australian palaeontologist Raymond Dart proved the scientific community wrong back in 1924. His discovery of the ancient hominin *Australopithecus africanus* showed that humans evolved in Africa. It was previously believed that humans had evolved in Europe or Asia. So who knows? Maybe it's just a matter of time before someone unearths convincing proof that a yowie-like species really does – or did – exist. Maybe it'll be you who makes the discovery!

DROP BEARS

They look like cuddly koalas, but these vicious meat-eating animals are said to drop out of trees onto their prey. Is there truth behind the legend? Or is the whole thing just a joke invented to tease tourists?

The koala's evil twin

Drop bears are the size of leopards and weigh over 100 kilograms. To give you a sense of perspective, normal koalas weigh only around ten kilograms. Other than their size, drop bears look a lot like koalas. Except for their big pointy teeth, that is. Drop bears sport a serious set of incisors, built for slashing their prey's throat and ripping at their flesh. That's because, unlike the much-loved leaf-eaters, drop bears are carnivores. They feed on small mammals ... and sometimes even large ones.

Photographic evidence is difficult to obtain, but this recreation gives just a hint of the drop bear's vicious power.

Habitat and prey

According to the Australian Museum's website, the scientific name for the drop bear is *Thylarctos plummetus*. Drop bears are said to live in dense forests and open woodlands, mostly in the Great Dividing Range that stretches across south-eastern Australia. They have also been spotted in other mountainous regions throughout the country. Drop bears tend to shy away from busy roads and residential areas. This is lucky for us, as these fantastic creatures are ambush predators. A hungry drop bear will wait patiently in a tree, looking much like a sleeping koala until its prey passes underneath. Then – *whomp*! It drops on top of its unfortunate victim. The impact is often enough to stun the prey, which is then quickly killed with a bite to the neck. Small prey is dragged back up the tree where it can be eaten in peace.

Dangers to humans

The Australian Museum notes that bushwalkers have been attacked by drop bears. Bites and other serious injuries have been sustained, but according to official statistics, there are no known human fatalities.

Or so we are told. Government officials refuse to admit that drop bears even exist. Is this because they're worried it might hurt our tourism industry? Australia relies on the money that comes from tourists enjoying our unspoilt wilderness. If they knew the truth about drop bears, they might be afraid to come, and the Australian economy would suffer. Then again, tourists aren't put off by our deadly snakes, spiders, sharks, blue-ringed octopuses, box jellyfish, stingrays or high UV levels, so maybe drop bears wouldn't worry them after all.

It's important to be on the lookout for drop bears while bushwalking. Keep an eye out for these signs!

DANGER! NEXT 300km

So what should we, as patriotic Australians, do? Should we uphold the silence or should we warn visitors? Perhaps the best approach is to give overseas tourists a few tips on how to protect themselves from drop bears, just in case!

Drop bear survival tips

Experts at the University of Tasmania carried out a scientific study to learn more about the drop bear. The results were published in the highly regarded *Australian Geographic* magazine. The study found that overseas tourists are more likely to be targeted than locals. The reasons for this are twofold. First, drop bears are able to detect Australian accents. Apart from learning how to mimic us, there isn't much useful advice for the tourist here. But as for the second reason ... Drop bears are repelled by the smell of Vegemite. Australians who eat Vegemite regularly exude it from their skin. As tourists don't, they are advised to smear the paste liberally behind their ears and under their armpits. Wearing forks in the hair is also recommended.

And yes, this is a real study! You can find the reference in 'Want more?' on page 44. Feel free to forward the link to anyone who doesn't believe you, particularly if they live overseas. Just make sure you don't point out that the article was published on 1 April – April Fools' Day!

THE HAWKESBURY RIVER MONSTER

Most people have heard of Scotland's Loch Ness monster. But did you know the legendary Nessie might have a cousin Down Under?

A local addition to the legend

Snake-like head. Long neck and body. Powerful tail. Massive flippers. Lives in the water. Sound familiar? This is how countless witnesses have described the Loch Ness monster. It's also the description of Australia's own Hawkesbury River monster. Northwest of Sydney, the Hawkesbury River is surrounded by scenes of natural beauty and has long been a popular tourist destination. Visitors flock to view the stunning waterways, national parks and historic towns along the river. But according to rumours, some people have seen far more than they anticipated!

Several sightings of mysterious aquatic creatures swimming below or alongside boats in the Hawkesbury River have been reported. Sightings going back many decades were often linked with capsized or missing boats. There are also centuries-old paintings made by Indigenous Australians that seem to depict the monsters. Although local reports of the monster are nowhere near as common as they are in Scotland, there are certainly enough to make people sit up and take notice.

Australian cryptozoologist Rex Gilroy is convinced a river monster lurks beneath the deep waters of the Hawkesbury. With a decades-long fascination for the creature, he and his wife, Heather

Gilroy, are the authors of *Out of the Dreamtime: The Search for Australasia's Unknown Animals*. The book contains an entire chapter on the Hawkesbury River monster, as well as detailed information about other Australian cryptids. But these authors don't just write about mysterious creatures; they are seasoned investigators. They have interviewed countless witnesses and even claim to have spotted strange creatures themselves.

Sightings over the years

The Gilroys share their findings in their book and on their website, Mysterious Australia. (See 'Want more?' on page 44 for

Is there a Loch Ness monster swimming around Down Under?

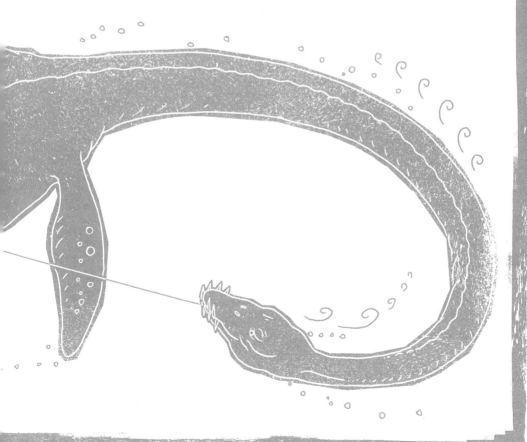

details.) One of the sightings they retell dates from 1949, when a young couple in a rowing boat were watching a bull drinking from the river. A large head on a long neck suddenly rose up six metres out of the water. The massive creature grabbed the bull and effortlessly pulled it under the water. When the couple told their story to the bull's owner, he wasn't sure what to make of it. He agreed, though, that he'd found marks of a struggle and blood on the sand. And the bull had most definitely vanished!

The Gilroys go on to recount a large number of sightings by fishermen, sightseers and people out on boats. There have been sightings not just of the monster itself, but also mysterious gigantic slide marks near the water, which looked as if they were made when the creature slithered out of the water to rest on the river banks. Rex Gilroy states that he has personally seen the monster through binoculars, and he has made it his life's mission to unearth convincing proof that the creature exists.

Zoologists are sceptical, however. They claim that the sightings are most likely of common creatures such as sharks or eels and that the reason they might look so big and strange is that the images were distorted by water or distance.

Ancient stories and artwork

In their defence, the Gilroys raise the traditional stories told by the Dharuk people of the New South Wales Central Coast, who spoke of water monsters inhabiting the river. The locals call this monster Mirreeulla, which means 'giant water serpent'. Their tales warn of women and children being attacked by the monster, and the Gilroys believe these stories originated from real experiences. The legendary stories were also the subject of ancient Indigenous cave art, showing a creature that looks a lot like Scotland's Loch Ness monster. The Gilroys don't think this is a coincidence! They believe that despite the great distance separating them, there is a link between the animals. Furthermore, they posit that the Loch Ness monster and the Hawkesbury River monster – and other similar monsters around the world – may be surviving examples of prehistoric marine reptiles. Sightings have been reported in places as far apart as Alaska, Japan and Russia. Previously thought extinct, have these creatures somehow managed to survive almost undetected into the modern day? The investigators say it is important to keep in mind the great length and depths of the Hawkesbury River. It has many branches snaking off it and, in their opinion, there is more than enough room for the creatures to have lived there undisturbed over the millennia.

A plesiosaur, perhaps?

Plesiosaurs weren't dinosaurs, but these massive marine creatures lived alongside them. Alive during the Jurassic and Cretaceous periods, they are commonly believed to have died out during the mass extinction that took place 65 million years ago. Plesiosaurs were long snaky-necked reptiles, 11 metres from head to tail. They seem to be an awfully close match to the description of the alleged river monsters! These fish-eating creatures lived in shallow seas. Fossils of plesiosaurs have been found in Australia, as well as Europe and North America. Is it possible that the species didn't die out, as was generally believed? Could a few pockets of plesiosaurs have continued to live and breed in remote areas across the globe?

In 2003, a scrap-metal dealer claimed to have literally stumbled upon a plesiosaur fossil on the banks of Loch Ness. The finding was confirmed by palaeontologists from the National Museum of Scotland, who also believed the man found it where he claimed he had. Even so, they didn't believe it proved Nessie existed. The experts thought the fossil had been deliberately planted by someone else as a hoax. This is because it didn't match the surrounding environment. Their examination showed it had existed in a marine environment and had been taken from a seashore. Loch Ness itself contains only fresh water.

The palaeontologists also pointed out that plesiosaurs were cold-blooded creatures, unlikely to have survived in the chilly Scottish loch. Mind you, the Hawkesbury River is much warmer ...

Are dinosaur-age plesiosaurs too large to live comfortably in the Hawkesbury River?

So you want to be a cryptozoologist?

This isn't the sort of thing you can study at university – mainly because cryptozoology is not a recognised field of science. But if you're interested, it would help to learn as much as possible about existing sciences, such as biology, zoology, chemistry and geology. Try doing volunteer work at a natural history museum or a zoo in order to learn more about your area of interest.

Good people skills are important, too, as much of your information will be gleaned from talking to eyewitnesses. Be prepared to camp out overnight in inhospitable environments as you search for the elusive beasts. You'll need reliable equipment such as a good pair of binoculars, visual and sound recorders, and scientific testing kits for analysing soil and other samples. You'll also need more than your fair share of courage! Encounters with cryptids can be frightening and even dangerous.

And, most importantly, you'll need to develop a thick skin. As thick, in fact, as that of a mythical mega-rhino. You'll need it because convincing other people of your beliefs will almost certainly be an uphill battle. But if you keep an open mind and arm yourself with hard facts, your discoveries might change the scientific world!

HOOP SNAKES

Not all snakes slither along the ground. According to some people, there are snakes that roll around like wheels! But is this true, or is it just an urban legend?

The fastest thing on one wheel

Hoop snakes have been reported throughout Australia, mostly in rural areas and in the outback. According to several witnesses, this snake grasps its tail in its mouth, forming a hoop shape. It then rolls after its prey at very high speeds. Once it reaches its prey the hoop snake unrolls, straightens itself, and strikes the victim down with deadly venom from its stinger tail. Rumour has it that the best way to outrun a hoop snake is to jump over a fence, as the snake is unable to climb over or roll through and follow. Diving through the hoop is also sometimes recommended as a way to escape, although it's not exactly clear why!

Zoologists don't believe hoop snakes exist. They argue that rolling is an unnatural way for animals to travel. It also goes against what they know about snake biology – it just doesn't seem physically possible for snakes to move in this way.

So how did the legend begin? Is it all just down to a writer's fertile imagination?

The cowboy connection

It seems that hoop snakes aren't purely an Australian phenomenon. They've been reported in other places as well, most notably in the United States. In the early 20th century, author Edward O'Reilly wrote a series of stories that featured deadly encounters with hoop snakes. Starring the cowboy Pecos Bill, the stories were set during the days of the American Wild West. The incredible Pecos Bill character was something of a legend – he used a rattlesnake as a lasso and another, smaller snake as a whip! It all sounds very fictional, so it stands to reason that the hoop snakes in the stories were perhaps made up too. But sightings of these peculiar snakes were around long before the tales were written. Is it possible the author had the rumours of these sightings in mind when writing his stories?

A tall tale – or a hooped tail?

Back in 1925, an article was published in *Natural History* magazine. Written by Karl Patterson Schmidt, an assistant curator at the Field Museum of Natural History, the article is titled 'The hoop snake story, with some theories of its origins'. In it Schmidt notes that the first written account of hoop snakes dates back to 1784, when a witness described a snake coiled into a circle and rolling rapidly. The snake apparently kept its tail pointed forward in the circle, ready to rapidly unroll itself and strike its victim down with its deadly fangs. This method of attack contradicts other reports, where hoop snakes were said to sting with their tail. This confusion could indicate that there are different types of hoop snakes – or it could simply mean witnesses were mistaken, perhaps due to their need to make a hasty retreat!

Before writing the article, the assistant curator had spoken to many people who claimed to have seen a hoop snake. Schmidt didn't want to suggest that these people were lying, yet he could find no credible evidence of hoop snakes beyond people's sightings. If hoop snakes existed, he thought, surely some specimens would have been found? He wondered whether the purported sightings might have been based on mud snakes. When held, these little snakes coil around the hand, forming a loop. Schmidt said this was a fairly normal habit of snakes that constrict their prey.

Real, not real – who knows? One thing is certain. If you ever do happen to see a hoop snake, look for a fence and jump over as fast as you can!

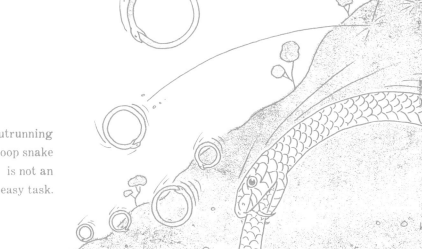

Outrunning a hoop snake is not an easy task.

$10,000 reward

Raymond Ditmars was a well-known naturalist and herpetologist. *Herpeton* is Greek for 'creeping animal', and herpetology is the study of reptiles and amphibians. If an animal creeps, crawls or slithers, herpetologists want to examine it. But what if the animal rolls? Ditmars was sceptical about the hoop snake's existence. Born in the late 19th century, Ditmars dedicated his life to the study of snakes. A zoo curator, he also wrote several books including *A Field Book of North American Snakes* and *Snakes of the World*.

Like any good researcher, Ditmars was open to being proved wrong. It is said he placed $10,000 in a New York bank account, to be awarded to the first person to prove hoop snakes exist.

Nobody has yet been able to claim the money.

It's probably not worth the effort of trying to find a hoop snake yourself, however. Poking around snakes is incredibly dangerous, especially Australian snakes!

Naturalist Raymond Ditmars offered a reward for convincing evidence that hoop snakes exist.

TASMANIAN TIGERS

The thylacine, also known as the Tasmanian tiger, is officially considered extinct. But many sightings have been reported – is it possible that it's still roaming around somewhere in the Australian wilderness?

The largest carnivorous marsupial in modern times

Unlike the animals previously discussed in this chapter, the Tasmanian tiger is not a cryptid. We know for sure that thylacines once existed. We even have surviving film footage of them. The mystery of the Tasmanian tiger revolves around whether they ever truly died out, as is commonly believed.

But first, what did a Tasmanian tiger look like? The animals were often described as looking rather like a cross between a dog and a kangaroo – they walked on

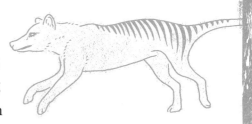

all fours and had the general appearance of a dog, but they had a big head and a heavy stiff tail like a kangaroo. They were sandy-brown to grey in colour and had distinctive dark stripes across their backs. Living in woodlands and grasslands, these semi-nocturnal creatures mainly hunted at night. Thylacines preyed on rodents, birds and other marsupials, including kangaroos and wallabies. After European colonisation, they also started to prey on sheep and poultry.

Although known as *Tasmanian* tigers, thylacines also used to live in mainland Australia. They were named Tasmanian tigers because they died out in the mainland long before they died out in Tasmania. Indigenous rock art depicts thylacines in various locations around Australia and fossils have been found in various parts of the country. It's thought that thylacines disappeared from the mainland around 3000 years ago. By the time of European settlement, thylacines were found only in Tasmania, and the very last one died in Tasmania in 1936.

So what killed them off? Their extinction might have been caused by the introduction of dingoes, who competed with them for food and habitat. Climate change has also been blamed, particularly the impact the climate had on their habitat and prey. One thing we know for sure that contributed to their decline was hunting. Thylacines were considered dangerous pests and a threat to farmers' livelihood. Although they did prey on sheep and poultry, it's possible that their reputation as livestock killers was exaggerated: some if not many of the kills were probably committed by foxes or feral dogs. A bounty was offered for the thylacine's slaughter and they were killed by the thousands, rapidly driving them to the point of extinction.

Movements to preserve the dwindling species started far too late. The last known thylacine was captured in the wild and kept in Hobart's Beaumaris Zoo, where it eventually died. But not before getting its revenge on humans. A cameraman filmed this last known thylacine – which promptly bit him on the bottom!

The last known living thylacine died in captivity in Hobart's Beaumaris Zoo in 1936.

Gone but not forgotten?

There have been literally thousands of sightings of animals thought to be Tasmanian tigers since 1936. And not just in Tasmania – the mainland gets its fair share of reports, too. Is it possible that they haven't completely died out after all?

Sightings are often made in areas where the habitat is suitable. Many of the reports are made by experienced farmers, who are confident they know the difference between thylacines and other animals. Thylacines had a very specific way of moving: slowly and stiffly. They had the very unusual ability to balance on their tail and stand on their hind legs like kangaroos. They also had a particular way of eating prey, sometimes only consuming the face and throat. And that's exactly what's being found today.

Could it be that there are still some wandering around? There are actually two types of extinction. Biological extinction occurs when a species is totally and permanently lost. Functional extinction means that a few survivors might still exist, but not enough to make the population sustainable. Could it be the case that the thylacine is functionally – rather than biologically – extinct?

Many photographs of supposed Tasmanian tigers have been sent for analysis. A large number were found to be mistaken, and were actually pictures of striped feral dogs. Some pictures have looked convincing but more hard evidence is needed before we conclude that the Tasmanian tiger is still around – evidence like footprints, hair and stool samples.

The hunt is on

Rumours of the existence of Tasmanian tigers were examined in the Australian television series *Animal X*, a show that investigated cryptids. The team, which included a zoologist and a conservationist, spoke to eyewitnesses and carried out investigations of their own. They were shown plaster casts of the unusual footprints of an animal with five toes. They explained that, in Australia, the only animal to have had five toes on its paws was the thylacine. The team even saw some fresh tracks matching this description.

Hidden cameras were set up in likely locations, but failed to provide any footage of thylacines. Still, just because they weren't caught on film, it doesn't mean they don't exist. Lots of animals that most certainly do exist didn't turn up on the film either!

Might there be a hidden agenda?

People make claims for many reasons. Hopefully they honestly believe them to be true — but sometimes there might be other motives at work.

The *Animal X* team considered a disturbing possibility. Many of the reported sightings of Tasmanian tigers were made in areas used for logging, such as Tasmania's Styx Valley. If thylacines were proved to exist there, logging would most likely be discontinued in an attempt to protect their habitat. This means there are strong financial motives for the logging industry to try to cover up any evidence of the thylacine that might exist.

Then again, the opposite could also be true. Some logging opponents might be tempted to go so far as to fake evidence of thylacines in the hope of stopping logging!

That doesn't imply this is the case here, mind you. It's just a reminder that it's always important to look behind, beneath and inside any argument before you believe what you hear!

Back from the dead

Can extinct animals ever be made un-extinct? It sounds like something out of a sci-fi movie. In the book and movie *Jurassic Park*, for example, dinosaurs were made un-extinct. This was done by extracting a dinosaur's DNA from a mosquito that had bitten the dinosaur and then been preserved in amber.

What began in a writer's vivid imagination is now becoming real scientific endeavour. A clone is an identical copy of a creature, and several living animals have been cloned already. This has been done by using their DNA, a set of molecules that contain the recipe for the creation of a species. Scientists are even confident they can clone a woolly mammoth, which became extinct thousands of years ago.

In 1999, the Australian Museum launched a project to clone a thylacine. The museum's idea was to use DNA from a thylacine pup that had been preserved in alcohol for nearly 136 years. Although they were able to recover DNA from the pup, its quality was too poor to work with. Sadly, the project had to be abandoned. There has been some progress since then, but it's unlikely that the thylacine will be brought back by cloning any time soon. A reminder that it's far better to prevent the extinction of a species than to try to reverse it!

Can the information found in DNA be used to bring back an extinct species?

WANT MORE?

For more information about these and other mythical creatures, have a look at:

- Dean Harrison's Australian Yowie Research website at http://www.yowiehunters.com.au

- Gilroy R & H, *Out of the Dreamtime: The Search for Australasia's Unknown Animals,* URU Publications, 2006 and their website at http://www.mysteriousaustralia.com

- Healy T & Cropper P, *The Yowie: in Search of Australia's Bigfoot*, Strange Nation, 2006

- Holden R, *Bunyips: Australia's Folklore of Fear*, National Library of Australia, 2001

- Middleton A, 'Drop bears target tourists, study says', *Australian Geographic*, 1 April 2013, retrieved from http://www.australiangeographic.com.au/news/2013/04/drop-bears-target-tourists,-study-says/

- Paddle R, *The Last Tasmanian Tiger: The History and Extinction of the Thylacine*, Cambridge University Press, 2002

- Image of original document describing a yowie, on the State Library of New South Wales website, at http://acms.sl.nsw.gov.au/item/itemLarge.aspx?itemID=98388

MYSTERIOUS LOCATIONS

Australia is such a large country, with such diverse landscapes. It shouldn't come as a surprise, then, that some very odd things happen here. From beautiful beaches to majestic mountains, rich rainforests to desiccated deserts, we've got it all. As the national anthem says, our land abounds in nature's gifts. Some of these gifts, however, are stranger than others!

Have you ever seen the ocean glow with eerie lights near Cairns, or watched mirages form in the Nullarbor? Perhaps you've paddled around the horizontal waterfalls in the Kimberley? While spectacular, these marvels are examples of natural phenomena. In other words, they can be explained by normal human experience or by science. The glowing sea at Cairns, for instance, is due to bioluminescence – a chemical reaction that takes place within living marine organisms.

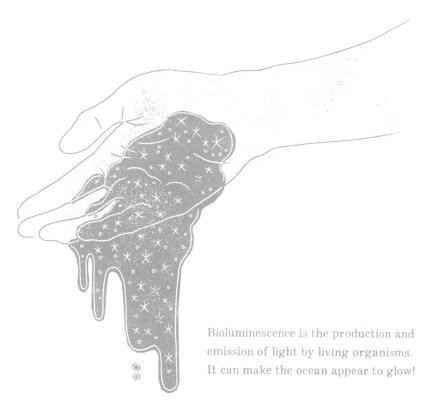

Bioluminescence is the production and emission of light by living organisms. It can make the ocean appear to glow!

Some things, however, are more difficult to explain. They are so bizarre that people can't agree on their causes. Stones falling from the sky in Western Australia. Mysterious moving lights in the outback. Unexplained disappearances in the Bass Strait. These events defy logic and appear to violate the rules of the natural world. Are they perhaps examples of *super*natural phenomena?

This may look like a human-made pavement, but the tessellated rock at Eaglehawk Neck, Tasmania, is a natural phenomenon.

Some people believe logical explanations for these mysteries do indeed exist, but haven't been discovered yet. Others insist there is no explanation. They believe the cause is beyond the natural realm – something other-worldly or spirit-driven.

What do you think? Not sure yet? Take a closer look at these mysterious locations and the unsettling things that happen there . . . If you dare!

THE FALLING STONES
OF MAYANUP

According to witnesses, stones plummeted from the sky in rural
Western Australia, seemingly coming from nowhere. What possible
explanation could there be?

A shower of stones

Rock and roll! No, we're not discussing the music of the 1950s,
we're talking about an incredible phenomenon that also occurred
around that time and into the 1960s: four isolated Western
Australian communities, all within 300 kilometres of each other,
reported mysterious stones falling from the sky.

According to the reports, most rocks stopped where they
landed, while others rolled small distances. Some people were hit
but fortunately not hurt. They said they were struck very softly, as
if the stones hadn't travelled far – or as if they had fallen slowly.

This is particularly strange, considering that objects falling under the force of gravity generally accelerate at a set rate: 9.8 metres per second squared. So rocks falling slower than that appear to be somehow defying gravity!

The rocks continued to fall over a period of weeks and months, even years in some places. The falls weren't continuous. There would be breaks, and then it would start all over again. Most falls took place at night, but falls during the day were also recorded.

The place that received the most media coverage was Mayanup, near the small Western Australian town of Boyup Brook. Initial reports of the falling stones came from Indigenous people who were camped in the area. They witnessed stones falling on paddocks, yet could see nobody who could have thrown them. Incredibly, stones also fell through tents, roofs and walls without leaving any holes! The stones were warm to the touch, and occasionally there were reports of other objects in the sites

of the rock falls – objects such as household items – moving or behaving mysteriously.

Farmers also witnessed stones falling on their properties, and news of the phenomenon spread. Tourists travelled long distances to see these falling rocks for themselves. Hundreds of independent witnesses confirmed the sightings, including hard-nosed news reporters.

Mischief makers, meteorites and more

So what might have caused the falling stones? In 2005, the ABC produced a documentary called *Spirit Stones*. Its overview report, *Explanations for the falling stones*, examined the possible causes.

The first thing that sprang to mind was practical jokers enjoying a laugh at other people's expense. Yet when the police were called in, they found no evidence of human involvement. Despite a rigorous investigation, the police were unable to unearth any pranksters.

One theory going around at the time was that the falling stones were actually showers of meteorites. This idea was knocked on the head, however, when geologists examined the composition of the stones. They concluded that they were not extraterrestrial. Rather, they were made of the same material as other stones in the area.

Could the phenomenon have been caused by freak weather conditions? Tornadoes can pick objects up and deposit them on the ground far from their source. But night after night after night? It doesn't seem likely. Furthermore, meteorological records from the time suggested that weather was not the cause. Geothermal activity – caused by heat under the Earth's surface – had also been flagged as a possible culprit, but again, no evidence was put forward to suggest that might have been the case.

A case of super-nature?

No natural cause has ever been identified, even after all these years. Which leads us to . . . supernatural causes! The Indigenous communities of the area felt the most closely connected to the phenomenon. They felt that the stones were related to their intimate connection with the spirit world. The documentary explored their story. In the film, Noongar elders reflected on the mysterious events and shared their thoughts on what might have caused the falling rocks. Some of the elders thought that spirits were responsible, and took steps to solve the problem. A ghost-laying ceremony was held in Mayanup to capture the spirit of a man who was ill and whose spirit was thought to have left his body. The ceremony succeeded, but the stones continued to fall. At Pumphrey's Bridge, a policeman recorded that some of the local Indigenous people attributed the falling stones to the Widgecarra, little men that could be heard but not seen. The Widgecarra were believed to get upset and become active when someone walked over the grave of an Indigenous person, which was considered a sign of disrespect.

Other people, however, suspected different types of spirits were to blame. Mischievous, energetic spirits, sometimes playful, sometimes malicious, out to cause distraction and even destruction. In a word: poltergeists. One person who came under scrutiny was a 14-year-old girl named Audrey. An experiment was performed in the presence of a large number of people and reported in the local newspaper. Each time Audrey was removed from her house, rocks fell. The stones were said to follow her wherever she went, even appearing in her bed. Was Audrey haunted by a poltergeist?

A noisy ghost?

Poltergeist is German for 'noisy ghost'. Poltergeist activity has been recorded throughout the centuries, across the world. They are said to be mischievous ghosts, generally harmless but sometimes acting with evil intent. Poltergeists are often associated with loud noises, such as rapping on walls and doors. They are said to make objects levitate and, if angered, may hurl them violently. The throwing of stones is not uncommon.

Poltergeists are believed to haunt or possess a particular person, rather than a place, which means that they don't remain in one location. Typically the poltergeist latches onto an adolescent female, usually one who's under physical or emotional stress. Perhaps the highly charged energy of a repressed and unhappy girl gives the poltergeist the chance it needs to manifest.

Many modern-day psychic investigators believe that poltergeist activity is not caused by a ghost, but rather by telekinesis. Telekinesis is the ability to move objects by the power of the mind. Girls experience massive hormonal changes as they go through puberty. Might this physical supercharge result in temporary telekinesis? On a subconscious level, perhaps, so that even the girl is unaware of what's going on? It sounds feasible. After all, poltergeist activity looks a lot like someone throwing a massive tantrum!

MiN MiN LiGHTS

Will-o'-the-wisps, jack-o'-lanterns, ghost lights . . . Many countries have stories of mysterious moving lights that can lead travellers into danger. Australians know them as Min Min lights, but what exactly are they?

First sighting

Australian UFO researcher Bill Chalker has explored many sightings of these strange lights. In *Australasian Ufologist Magazine*, he published an article called 'The Min Min light revealed: nature unbound?', where he explained how the stories originated.

According to legend, the first sighting of a Min Min light dates back to the 1880s, in the outback town of Boulia, Queensland. A stockman was riding his horse past the site of a small pub called the Min Min, which had burnt to the ground not long before. He saw a strange glowing light hovering above the ground in a nearby cemetery. The light was about the size of a small watermelon. Shockingly, the light moved and even began to follow him! It kept pursuing him until he reached the outskirts of town, when it suddenly vanished.

Not surprisingly, nobody believed the unfortunate stockman's story. Not until it started happening to others, that is. A few locals found the courage to come forward and report the same thing that the stockman had experienced. Since then, mysterious floating lights have been reported throughout the country. Regardless of location, they are still known as Min Min lights.

Sightings have been made by people who were considered unlikely to be persuaded by myths. Chalker described an article published in the *Royal Geographical Society of Australia Bulletin* in 1981. The article quoted a statement by Detective Sergeant Lyall Booth, who was camped overnight at a waterhole. DS Booth was awoken by a strange light hovering below tree height. He watched it throughout the night. It moved around to some extent and then kept still. Finally it dived rapidly towards the ground and went out.

Sightings continue to occur today, with people sometimes thinking the Min Min lights are merely car headlights. That's until the lights begin to bounce around in a most non-headlight kind of way. Or until they realise there is no car attached!

Eerie floating globes

So what do the Min Min lights look like? They have been described as either round or football-shaped. Generally only one appears at a time, although some people claim to have seen two or more. Sizes vary, but are typically similar to melons. Usually the lights are white, but other colours have also been reported. The lights can be close to the ground or above head height. They've been reported as keeping still or moving unpredictably – sometimes even giving chase.

Some people claim the lights give off a strange ozone smell, an odour that has been described as similar to electric sparks. Horses have been reported to become upset when the lights are present. Nowadays, drivers report static on their car radios. This makes it seem as if the lights might be related to an atmospheric disturbance . . . Or does it?

Possibilities

Local Indigenous elders have a spiritual explanation for the first Min Min light spotted by the stockman. They believe the light came from an old Indigenous burial ground, and only started appearing after the British arrived and began killing their people. Min Min lights may have belonged to spirits that had been angered by the deaths. Perhaps they were issuing a warning against further killings.

Glowing balls of light have been witnessed throughout the world by thousands of people, including scientists studying the phenomenon. The question is, what are they? Investigators have tried to find logical, natural explanations. Burning gas in marshes was once suspected, but this theory couldn't account

for sightings far from gas sources, and it also couldn't explain the odd movements the lights sometimes made. Some people have suggested that the lights might be clouds of glowing insects, but this would mean that the sphere of light would be likely to break up as the insects went their different ways, rather than suddenly vanish. A swarm of insects would also presumably make some noise, unlike the perfect silence of the Min Min lights.

Ball lightning has also been bandied about as a possibility. Ball lightning is the term used to describe glowing orbs of light that sometimes form during storms. The size of a grapefruit, they can jerk around erratically before disappearing. It's an interesting idea, but it doesn't explain why Min Min lights are seen under calm weather conditions.

Is this sign for tourists a warning – or an invitation?

Fairy lights

Professor John Pettigrew of the University of Queensland may have found the answer. A director of the university's Vision, Touch and Hearing Research Centre, he personally witnessed the lights several times while on field trips. He claimed the lights aren't mystical, rather that they can be explained by an interplay of factors.

First, there must be a light source, which is either natural (for example a star or planet) or human-made (such as a car headlight). This light is then refracted – or bent – along great distances. This can happen under certain atmospheric conditions involving cold, dense layers of air near the ground.

The phenomenon is known as an inverted mirage. But even this sober explanation has a dash of the creative. It's also known as a Fata Morgana – named after the wicked sorceress Morgan le Fay. According to the legends of King Arthur, Morgan conjured images of fairy castles on the sea, luring sailors to their deaths!

HANGING ROCK

The 1967 book *Picnic at Hanging Rock* by Joan Lindsay haunts people to this day. Did a group of schoolgirls and a teacher mysteriously vanish at the rock, or was it all part of an author's feverish imagination?

It's no picnic!

A film version of the book was released in 1975, bringing the eerie story to a much wider audience. Set in 1900, the action begins in a genteel boarding school for girls called Appleyard College. A Valentine's Day excursion is arranged to Hanging Rock, which is a real place in the Macedon Ranges north of Melbourne. Filled with panpipe music, the atmospheric film takes the creepy feel of the book to new heights.

Odd things happen during the picnic. For instance, the teachers' watches stop working at noon, just before the story takes a dark turn. Four students decide to separate from the others to go

for a walk. They continue to walk, smiling and happy, but before long a change comes over the girls. They become serious and grim and determined to keep going – all except for one worried student who wants to turn back and rejoin the group. She is ignored by the other three. In a hypnotic trance, they take off their stockings and shoes (quite shocking in those days!) and climb the rock. This is despite warnings to be on the lookout for venomous snakes and vicious biting ants.

When the girls don't come back, a teacher goes to look for them. She, too, never returns. Only the reluctant fourth girl manages to make her way back, hysterical and unable to explain what has happened. After days of searching, one of the missing three girls is finally found. Unconscious and close to death, she is unable to shed light on the mystery. There is something peculiar about her, however. Her clothes and fingernails are bloodied and torn, but her bare feet are clean and unscratched. Most peculiar of all, her corset is missing!

According to the film and book, the police investigation ruled out foul play. There was no sign that the girls had been abducted or assaulted. This led countless fans to ask: what happened? Theories ranged from avalanches to alien abductions. But the real answer is even more startling. Nothing happened! Nope, nothing at all. Although many people aren't aware of it, the story is pure fiction.

Why do so many people think it's true?

So why, then, do so many people think the story of the picnic at Hanging Rock is true? Partly it's because the location is real, and it has been reported by many people as having an eerie feeling

Author Joan Lindsay, c. 1925.

about it. It also helps that the story was set before living memory, so no one is around to say what the book and film describe never happened.

But perhaps the strongest reason people persist in thinking the story is true is that the publisher and author actively encouraged this belief. The novel was written as if it were a true story, and the prologue and epilogue read as if they are relating historical fact. Joan Lindsay herself was cagey during interviews. When asked if the story was true, she said that she preferred readers to make up their own minds. Clever, that.

Inconsistencies and hints

There were some clues, however, that all was not as it seemed. 14 February 1900 was described as a Saturday in the film and book. A quick Google search shows that date was actually a Wednesday. Maybe that's not such a big deal, but there's more. Appleyard College never existed. Try searching the characters' names: no results will come up showing real people connected to the story. And it wasn't just a case of names being changed to keep identities secret. The disappearances themselves were never reported by the press or investigated by the police. Fans who flock to libraries keen to research the mystery are sadly disappointed – there is nothing to research!

The final chapter

When the novel was originally published, the final chapter was removed from the book. Chapter 18, written as a flashback, actually solved the story's mystery, but in a clever move, the editor and author agreed it shouldn't be published until after Joan Lindsay's death. Even after her death, though, most people didn't know this chapter existed!

It was released in 1987, three years after the author died, under the title *The Secret of Hanging Rock.* And so the mystery is over! Ready for the solution?

The chapter opens with the three girls feeling dizzy and falling asleep – the fourth had run back by then. They wake when their exhausted teacher finally finds them. The girls remove the teacher's corset so she can breathe more easily (corsets were extremely tight). They also remove their own and toss them over the cliff. But ... they don't fall! The corsets remain hanging in midair and the teacher suggests that they are suspended in time.

A hole in space then appears. A brown snake disappears through a crack in the rock, and the teacher suggests they follow it. She turns into a lizard and slips through the crack. Two of the girls do the same, but before the third can follow, a boulder tilts and blocks the hole. The story ends with the surviving girl beating and scratching at the rock with her bare hands, unable to follow the others. This explains the state of her hands and nails when she is eventually found.

Remember, the whole story is fiction. If the final chapter had been published from the beginning, this would have been clear and the eerie legend would never have been born.

THE DEVIL'S POOL

For some reason, a large number of young men have drowned in the Devil's Pool at Babinda Boulders in Cairns. Are the deaths caused by natural forces, or are they related to an ancient Indigenous legend?

Dangerous waters

Babinda means 'water flowing over rocks' in the local Indigenous language, and it's certainly an apt description of the Babinda Boulders in far north Queensland. Known as the Devil's Pool, one section of this waterway is a torrent of crashing, foaming waves. It's the scene of at least 16 recorded deaths – virtually all young men. The unofficial number of deaths over the years is thought to be even higher.

What is the reason for all these deaths? Clearly these are dangerous waters, characterised by slippery rocks, swirling currents and hidden channels. Even strong swimmers caught in

The rough waters of the Devil's Pool have claimed the
lives of many young men.

these waters would have difficulty escaping. But why is it just young
men that drown? Is it because they might be more reckless, or is
there another reason? Another mysterious question remains, too:
why is it only visitors who drown, not the people who live there?

An ancient tragedy

The local Indigenous people have a deep spiritual understanding of this mysterious place. They shared their story in the ABC
television show *Message Stick*, a program about Aboriginal and
Torres Strait Islander lifestyles, culture and issues. In the Babinda
Boulders episode, Yidinji elder Annie Wonga shared an ancient
legend. A story of romance, passion and sacrifice . . .

According to the Yidinji people, long ago a beautiful young
woman called Oolana was given to a wise elder named Waroonoo

in marriage. They had a big dance to celebrate the wedding. While this was taking place, a wandering tribe passed through their land. As was the custom with the Yidinji, the visitors were made welcome. In this visiting tribe was a handsome young man called Dyga. It was love at first sight for Oolana and Dyga. While they danced, their feelings grew. They ran away together further up the creek, where they camped overnight.

The next morning, the two tribes came searching for them. Dyga was seized by his people, who said he had brought shame upon them. They would leave and never return. Heartbroken, Oolana threw herself into the creek. There was a great upheaval in the once-gentle waters. Huge boulders were thrown up, and the water surged with the violent passion of her emotions. Legend has it that her spirit remains there to this day, calling out to her lover. Wandering travellers must take care not to answer her call, or they might stay with her forever.

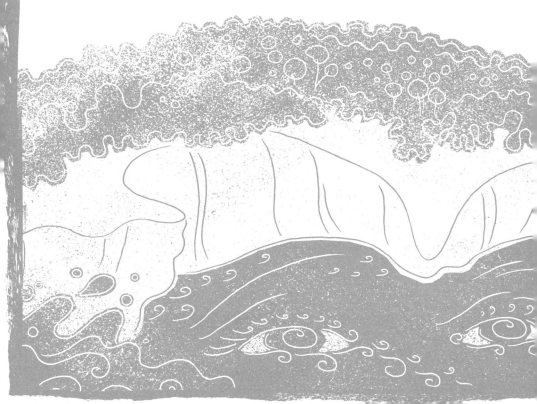

Continuing tragedies

In the show *Message Stick*, the locals explained that their young men swam in the pool regularly, yet were untouched. They believed something was protecting them. They said it felt as though an aura surrounded them and their friends as they swam.

This aura does not extend to people making a mockery of the legend, however. Respect for the story of Oolana is very important to the locals and, understandably, they become distressed when visitors show disrespect. As they pointed out in the documentary, every stone, every bone, every shell has meaning and value.

They described a recent death that occurred at the Devil's Pool. A visiting youth was dressed inappropriately and acting disrespectfully. He kicked at a bronze plaque commemorating the death of a previous victim. This caused him to slip into the same spot where the previous boy had, quickly becoming a victim himself.

Is an ancient tragedy being replayed in this mysterious place?

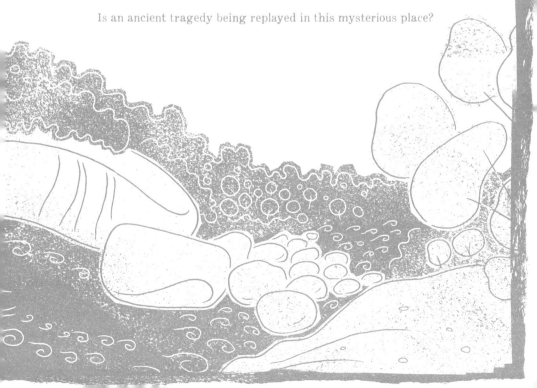

A matter of respect

Australia has a thriving nature-tourism industry. Unfortunately, it has often caused harm to the beautiful spots that people are so keen to see. Ecotourism operators strive to protect the environment – but this is only part of the problem. Often the wishes of Indigenous Australians are disregarded. The most famous example is Uluru, previously known as Ayers Rock. Climbing the rock is not prohibited, but the local Indigenous people consider it disrespectful because for them it is a sacred site.

There's a growing awareness of the benefits of cultural tourism. Cultural tours allow visitors to hear the fascinating stories of the local people's ancestral pasts. Each group has its own Dreaming stories, its own solutions to the challenges of everyday life. Being able to hear the unique experiences of Indigenous Australians enhances any visit and grounds it firmly within Australia's cultural history.

The ROC (Respecting Our Culture) tour certification was developed by Aboriginal Tourism Australia and is administered by Ecotourism Australia. It allows visitors to select tours that offer a cultural experience authenticated by local Indigenous people. Keep an eye out for the logo next time you plan to explore the country!

LASSETER'S REEF

No, not a coral reef – but a reef of gold! Did prospector Harold Lasseter really discover untold wealth in the Australian outback? If so, where is it? And why hasn't it been found to this day?

The legend begins

Not all myths are spooky. The legend of Lasseter's Reef isn't one bit scary, but it's still one of Australia's most puzzling mysteries. It might never be solved, but that's certainly not for lack of trying!

Lewis Hubert Lasseter was born in 1880, later changing his name to Lewis Harold Bell Lasseter. He was a prolific inventor, whose ideas mostly failed to take hold. Even his claim to be the original designer of the Sydney Harbour Bridge wasn't taken seriously. In many ways, he was a man before his time. Perhaps, if he had been born later, advances in technology might have allowed his creative ideas to become reality. But Lasseter is best known for the reef (a jagged ridge just under the surface) of gold he purportedly discovered in central Australia in 1897, when he was only 17 years old.

According to most accounts, Lasseter claimed to have stumbled across the reef while travelling through the Northern Territory's MacDonnell Ranges. Some of the gold glistened in the sunlight and was clearly visible, but once he started to dig he found there was far more than met the eye. Bulging with gold, the reef would have made him rich beyond his wildest dreams. Unfortunately he became hopelessly lost while making his way back to civilisation. Even so, he was confident he could find his way back to the reef one day.

Lasseter's expedition

It took Lasseter many years to go public with his find, and that in itself caused many to doubt him. Most people refused to take him seriously, but in 1930 he managed to convince an influential supporter to set up an expedition to search for the reef. This was during the Great Depression, mind you, when huge numbers of people were unemployed, and the promise of gold shone brighter than ever. The risk was worth it! Lasseter was hired as a paid guide and they set off into the desert.

Lasseter's supporters started to lose faith in him when he failed to find anything. Lasseter himself was accused of being uncooperative and sulky. Hardships and arguments took the gloss off the expedition. Sand dunes blocked the way and the truck the group travelled in became stuck many times. When they reached terrain that was virtually impassable, the members of the expedition finally decided to stop and turn back.

Lasseter refused to give up on his dream, and such confidence might suggest it wasn't all a scam. He vowed to continue

Lasseter was guided by familiar landmarks, rather than geographically specific bearings.

searching, and was helped by a camel owner named Paul Johns who was not part of the original expedition. Unfortunately, they too quarrelled. As they neared their goal, Lasseter left Johns with the camels while he wandered off alone. When he returned he jubilantly claimed to have found the gold. He even said he had a sample in his pocket! He refused to say where the reef was, however, and even more strangely he refused to show Johns the sample. The bond of trust between the two men snapped like a twig. A shaky truce was eventually reached, and Johns was sent back to break the good news of the discovery. Meanwhile, Lasseter headed back to the reef, intending to take bearings and mark the site with pegs. He had only two camels to support him in the wilderness.

Sadly, tragedy struck.

Death in the desert

Perhaps Lasseter would have made it and become a very, very rich man – if his camels hadn't bolted, taking his food and water with them. According to Lasseter's diary, which was later found, he was stranded, alone and without provisions.

At times the local Indigenous people helped him, but at other times they didn't trust him and kept their distance. Lasseter lived in a cave and grew weaker and weaker. He spent his final days writing in his diary. In it he stated that he had found the reef again, and that he had pegged out the location. He drew a map and stated that the reef was near a sacred Indigenous place. That may explain – at least partly – why the locals were wary of him. Bringing all that unwanted attention into their sacred places would have been intolerable. It is possible that Lasseter himself – perhaps unknowingly – was interfering with a sacred site.

Starving and close to death, Lasseter went on to say in his diary that although he'd found the gold, he'd 'give it all for a loaf of bread'. A tragic end to a lifelong dream!

A camel team was sent out to search for Lasseter. His body and his diary were recovered.

The legend continues

The law presumes that, unless something shows otherwise, people are unlikely to lie when they know they're close to death. Does this apply here? To the last, Lasseter maintained the existence of the gold reef. Does this mean that it truly does exist? Or could Lasseter's dying words in his diary be a bunch of lies? If so, why did he do it? He knew his chance of rescue was slim, yet he stuck to his story. Might he simply have been mistaken?

Since Lasseter's death, countless people have tried to find the gold reef. There have been many expeditions into the remote wilderness, but so far none have turned up anything promising. Any pegs that might have been planted decades ago are likely to have blown away or become covered in sand.

Harold Lasseter's son Bob made a lifelong commitment to find his father's treasure. He has personally searched the area many times, despite the harsh conditions and his advancing age. In 2013, aged 85, he appeared in a documentary called *Lasseter's Bones*. Bob Lasseter and the documentary presenter, Luke Walker, tried to retrace Lasseter's steps and track down the gold. The difficulty of such a task in a large, unforgiving country was made only too clear. The dedicated son appears to be driven not so much by wealth ... but by the chance to vindicate his father and put the rumours to rest. Will the truth ever be known?

THE BASS STRAIT TRIANGLE

Just like the better-known Bermuda Triangle, a large number of ships and aircraft have inexplicably vanished in the Bass Strait. What could the reason possibly be?

Without trace

The Bass Strait is the waterway that separates Tasmania from mainland Australia. The so-called Bass Strait Triangle lies underneath Victoria, with its base sweeping across the north coast of Tasmania. Many ships and planes have vanished without a trace in these waters.

The particularly famous disappearance of Frederick Valentich in 1978 led to the Strait's nickname, echoing the name of the mysterious Bermuda Triangle that lies off the south-eastern coast of the United States. You can read all about the Valentich mystery

on page 164. But the unexplained disappearances in the strait started long before that!

In his book *Mysteries of the Bass Strait Triangle*, Jack Loney noted that the disappearances date back to the early days of colonisation. The first recorded victim of the Bass Strait Triangle was the longboat *Eliza*. On 21 June 1797, she left Sydney to help recover cargo from a wrecked ship. The longboat disappeared into the strait and was never seen again. Dozens more sea vessels of all shapes and sizes were soon to follow suit: schooners, cutters, full-rigged ships and steamships. Sometimes bits of wreckage were found washed up on shores, at other times the vessels vanished completely. Tragically, yachts competing in the annual Sydney to Hobart yacht race have also been lost or wrecked in these waters, even in recent times.

One particularly odd 19th-century case was that of the cutter *Elsie May*. In May 1897 she was found drifting within the triangle. She was filled with water but with sails set. There was no trace of her crew, and nobody knew what might have caused them to abandon ship.

Was it something in the water? Maybe, but that wouldn't explain the loss of aircraft that followed in the 20th century. In 1920, experienced pilot Captain Stutt was sent to search for two ships that were thought to have gone missing in the strait: the *Amelia J* and the *Southern Cross*.

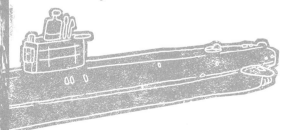

The captain's de Havilland 9A biplane was in good condition, and he flew alongside another search plane. The two

A de Havilland 9A biplane, like the one that went missing in
the Bass Strait in 1920.

planes became separated in clouds, however, and Captain Stutt
was never seen again. Sadly, many light planes have been lost in
the strait over the years.

It wasn't just small aircraft that came to grief in the triangle's
airspace. In 1934 the four-engined DH 86 commercial airliner
Miss Hobart radioed 'Everything okay' before vanishing forever.
The next year, a similar disaster occurred and again, no reason
was found. What could be causing all these tragedies?

Violent nature or super-nature?

Time warps, reverse-gravity fields and holes in space are all ideas
that have been put forward to explain disappearances in the
Bermuda Triangle. As with the Bermuda Triangle, there has been
much speculation over the forces at work in the Bass Strait. What
are people saying about the triangle Down Under?

There have been whispers of giant monsters and sea serpents. There have also been stories of mysterious whirlpools appearing out of nowhere, sucking ships down into the watery depths of the ocean. Giant waves rising without warning and overwhelming sea vessels are another possibility.

A more colourful suggestion – and one that is surprisingly plausible – is that of pirates. Pirates prowled Australian waters in the 19th century. There are stories of them lighting fires on deserted shorelines to lure ships, then killing and robbing everyone on board. Pirate activity was particularly common during the gold-rush days, and for many hopefuls, Bass Strait was the route to and from the goldfields. Indeed, the clipper *Madagascar* entered the strait in 1853 carrying large amounts of gold dust, before vanishing forever. Rumours that she was taken by pirates persisted for many years. But even if this was the cause of the disappearance of the ships in the Bass Strait, it doesn't explain the disappearance of the aeroplanes.

In his book, Jack Loney discussed his own theories. He claimed that many, if not most, of the disappearances could be explained by natural causes. The area has notoriously strong southerly and westerly winds. Combined with a shallow sea bottom, these winds can lead to tall waves and confusing swells. Loney stated that most of the tragedies were probably caused by storms, tidal waves, pirates and human error. Unseaworthy vessels may also have been to blame. As for the aircraft, high winds, poor visibility and atmospheric conditions may have been the culprits. Loney's reasoning seems sound, but the debate continues nonetheless.

Bass himself vanished

There's another interesting thing to note about the Bass Strait. It was named after the famous explorer George Bass. In 1798 to 1799, George Bass and Matthew Flinders circumnavigated Tasmania, which was then called Van Diemen's Land. You probably knew that. But did you know that George Bass himself disappeared?

No, not in the triangle. That would make a good story, though! Even so, Bass' disappearance is a mystery in itself.

In February 1803 Bass set sail for South America, which was then Spanish territory. He left to go on a private trading mission, hoping to pay off his debts and strike it rich. His ship *Venus* was lost during this voyage, never to be seen again. No one knows what happened. One theory was that he and his crew were captured by the Spanish and arrested as smugglers. If so, Bass may well have died working as a slave in the South American silver mines.

Death of an environmentalist

In 1972, the green movement was still in its infancy. Environmental activists were considered more of a pest than a serious political force. But this didn't stop Brenda Hean taking a stand against a hydro-electric scheme in Tasmania. The scheme required the flooding of picturesque Lake Pedder. Large sums of money were at stake and emotions ran high. Despite death threats, Hean and pilot Max Price took off in a tiny biplane to go to Canberra to lobby politicians. They planned to write 'Save Lake Pedder' in the sky above the capital city. Their route to Canberra took them over the Bass Strait.

They never arrived. The little plane and its passengers were never found.

The alarm was first raised when they failed to arrive at Flinders Island in Bass Strait to refuel. The night before the plane took off, its hangar was broken into, yet nothing had been stolen. Could this have been a case of sabotage? Given that the plane wreckage hasn't been recovered, it's impossible to say.

Mystery continues to surround the disappearance. Why didn't the pilot activate the emergency beacon? Was this a tragic accident? The result of deadly tampering? Or was it something else? Something supernatural? The Bass Strait Triangle isn't about to volunteer a solution just yet!

WANT MORE?

For more information about these mysterious Australian locations, have a look at:

- Hack H, *The Mystery of the Mayanup Poltergeist,* Hesperian Press, 2000

- Kozicka MG, *The Mystery of the Min Min Lights,* Bolton Imprint, 1994

- Lindsay J, *Picnic at Hanging Rock,* Penguin, 1967 (novel)

- Loney JK, *Mysteries of the Bass Strait Triangle,* Neptune Press, 1980

- Testa A, *A Dead Man's Dream: Lasseter's Reef Found,* Hesperian Press, 2005

- Wonga A, A Yidinji elder, tells the story of the Devil's Pool at http://aso.gov.au/titles/tv/message-stick-babinda-boulders/clip2/

HAUNTED
PLACES

Australia has no shortage of haunted places. Convict settlements, old gaols, theatres, psychiatric hospitals. Many historic sites are rumoured to be inhabited by ghosts, and this seems to be the case especially if ghastly things once happened there. There are hundreds if not thousands of reports every year of hazy visions and eerie sounds. Objects moving by themselves. Shadows. Feelings of dread and despair.

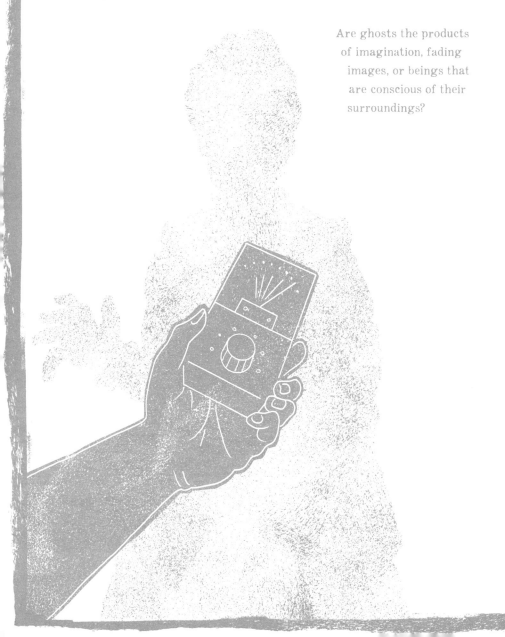

Are ghosts the products of imagination, fading images, or beings that are conscious of their surroundings?

But what actually is a ghost? No one knows for sure. Sceptics insist ghosts don't exist. They claim that ghosts are the product of wishful thinking and/or overactive imaginations. But maybe these sceptics just haven't ever come across one themselves! Or if they have, perhaps they rationalise it away. It was the wind howling. A trick of the light. Vibrations from another room.

People who believe in ghosts and think they've seen one seem to have a different world view. They can't always explain it, but they believe they saw *something*. Something that can't be understood by logic or science. They could, of course, be mistaken. Perhaps in some cases it really *was* the wind or a trick of the light. But does this mean all believers are deluded? If some people are mistaken, is everybody?

It isn't possible to definitively state there's no such thing as the supernatural. Just because we can't prove something exists, that doesn't mean it doesn't. Assuming, for the moment, that there are such things as ghosts, how can we explain what a ghost is?

One possibility is that they are echoes from the past. Some event – perhaps a traumatic death – caused those echoes to become imprinted in time, rather like a photograph or piece of film. Under the right circumstances the imprint is visible to people sensitive enough to tune in. If this is the case, ghosts are like images being played back on a screen. They are unaware of us watching them, which is creepy, but not exactly threatening.

Another possibility is much more frightening. Many suspected hauntings begin when people change things: an old building is modernised, a valued possession is removed. What if ghosts are the spirits of dead people, left to wander the earth? Maybe the spirits are aware; maybe they know what they are.

And they know who we are and they are watching us. And . . . maybe they're angry!

The study of ghosts comes under the heading of para-normal research, 'para' meaning 'beyond'. Professional ghost hunters often use psychics to help them investigate haunted places, relying on their ability to sense the dead and/or communicate with them. Senses and feelings are very subjective, however, and it's hard for anyone to prove or disprove what another person is experiencing. Therefore, many investigators also use scientific methods in their investigation of ghosts. They take readings of temperatures, vibra-tions and sounds and try to look for rational explanations for what they might be experiencing, such as doors leaning awkwardly on hinges, causing them to shut by themselves. Many supposed hauntings have turned out to be the result of identifiable natural causes. *But not all.* Read on to discover some of Australia's most haunted spots for yourself.

Before you decide to set off on a spot of ghost hunting, however, keep this in mind. In cases of private property, trespass-ing is strictly forbidden. And if the law doesn't get you, something else might!

COCKATOO ISLAND

With a history this horrifying, it's no surprise that Cockatoo Island is said to be haunted. Doors open and close for no apparent reason. Disembodied voices echo in the stillness of the night. Apparitions appear without warning. But who might be doing the haunting? And why?

A horrendous history

The largest island in Sydney Harbour has a long and violent past. Initially it was used by Indigenous people for canoe building and fishing. But in 1839, the governor of New South Wales decided to turn this spot of natural beauty into an imposing prison island. At that time, secondary offenders (convicts who continued to commit crimes after being transported to New South Wales as punishment for an earlier crime) were being sent to distant Norfolk Island. But Norfolk Island was becoming increasingly overcrowded. A new location was needed.

Cockatoo Island was seen as ideal because it was close to the settlement but separated by waters the prisoners believed to be shark-infested. A perfect deterrent for anyone trying to escape!

Life for the Cockatoo Island convicts was harsh. They were given the backbreaking task of quarrying sandstone for building projects in the colony. They also had to develop the island itself. Convicts hand-chiselled silos (circular chambers used to store grain) out of the bedrock, and built a dock while standing in water wearing leg irons. They even had to build their own cells and dungeons. Living conditions were appalling, and the prison was finally shut down in 1869.

But that's not the end of the story. Soon afterwards, the island became a girls' reformatory – a home for unruly and orphaned children. It offered little comfort to the new residents. Mistreated on a daily basis, the girls had to drink water out of a trough and eat without cutlery. Not only did this restrict the type of food they were able to eat, it was dehumanising, treating the girls as if they were animals. Punishments for misbehaviour were swift and severe and included beatings. The reformatory was run by a man called George Lucas (nothing to do with *Star Wars*). His wife, Mary Ann, was known for her controlling nature and red-hot rage.

The reformatory didn't last long. It was shut down in 1879 and the girls were moved to a new facility. The island reverted to being a public gaol, housing both male and female prisoners. The prison finally shut down for good when Sydney's Long Bay Gaol opened in 1909.

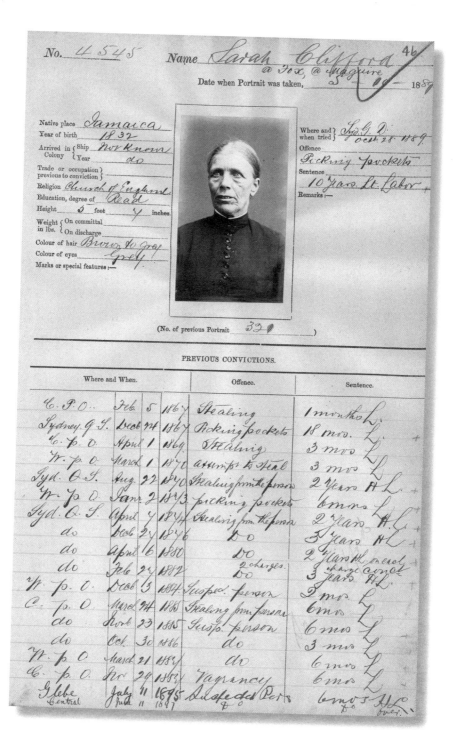

No. **4545** Name **Sarah Clifford** 46
a **Fox**, a **Maguire**
Date when Portrait was taken, **5 ___ — 188**9

Native place **Jamaica**
Year of birth **1832**
Arrived in Colony { Ship **Not Known**
{ Year **do**
Trade or occupation previous to conviction }
Religion **Church of England**
Education, degree of **Read**
Height **5** feet **4** inches
Weight in lbs. { On committal ___
{ On discharge ___
Colour of hair **Brown to Grey**
Colour of eyes **Grey**
Marks or special features :—

Where and when tried } **Syd G.D. Octr 28 1889**
Offence **Picking Pockets**
Sentence **10 Years Lt Labor**
Remarks :—

(No. of previous Portrait **320**)

PREVIOUS CONVICTIONS.

Where and When.				Offence.	Sentence.
C. P. O.	Feb	5	1867	Stealing	1 months L.
Sydney Q.S.	Decr 24		1867	Picking pockets	18 mos L.
C. P. O.	April 1		1869	Stealing	3 mos L.
W. P. O.	March 1		1870	attempt to steal	3 mos L.
Syd. Q.S.	Aug. 22		1870	Stealing from the person	2 Years H.L.
W. P. O.	Janr 2		1873	picking pockets	6 mos L.
Syd. Q.S.	April 7		1874	Stealing from the person	2 Years H.L.
do	Decr 24		1876	Do	3 Years H.L.
do	April 6		1880	Do	2 Years H.L. on each charge conct
do	Feb 24		1882	Do 2 charges.	3 Years H.L.
W. P. O.	Decr 13		1884	Suspd. person	3 mo L
C. P. O.	March 24		1885	Stealing from persons	6 mos L
do	Novr 23		1885	Suspd. person	6 mos L
do	Oct 30		1886	do	3 mos L
W. P. O.	March 21		1887	do	6 mos L
C. P. O.	Nov 29		1887	Vagrancy	6 mos L
Glebe	July 11		1895	Suspected Pers	6 mos LC
Central	July 11		1897	do	do HLC over.

The severity of penal life is reflected in the face of prisoner Sarah Clifford.

After that, Cockatoo Island gained a new lease of life as a naval dockyard, and was central to Australia's war effort. Shipbuilding continued on site right up until 1992. There was some debate about the island's fate, and in 2007 it was opened to the public. Now on the World Heritage List, it has become a popular tourist destination. It's visited by history lovers, families, school groups . . . and people keen to know if the horrific rumours are true . . .

The hauntings

Cockatoo Island has been described as one of the most haunted locations in Sydney. Many visitors have reported seeing menacing apparitions and hearing unearthly moans and cries. The island was even featured in an episode of *Haunting: Australia*, a popular TV show. The team investigated the island late at night, when tourists and visitors were safely off the premises.

The show identified a ghost called George, who has been said to haunt the officers' quarters on the island. While alive, George had been a convict sentry. Visitors to Cockatoo Island believe George continues to guard the staircase to the officers' quarters after his death, his footsteps audible as he marches unrelentingly up and down. In the Dog Leg tunnel, which winds its crooked way through the island, one of the show's ghost hunters saw a different spectre dressed as a naval captain striding along the walkway. The ghost hunter sensed that the apparition wasn't really that of an officer, but rather a prisoner dressed up while making an escape bid. Did the prisoner die there? Is he trapped in the tunnel for eternity, forever repeating his desperate bid for freedom?

There have also been other spectral sightings, but the most spine-chilling ghost would have to be the Red Lady: a woman

Is the spectre, once a prisoner attempting to escape,
trapped in the Dog Leg tunnel forever?

wearing a Victorian-style red dress. Many people claim to have seen the unhappy apparition gazing out of the windows of Biloela House, an old convict-built residence. The *Haunting: Australia* team speculated that she might be hot-tempered Mary Ann Lucas, wife of the reformatory overseer. What personal tragedy may have made the angry woman refuse to leave the island, even after her death?

The investigation

Like many other professional ghost busters, the *Haunting: Australia* team relied on scientific instruments to make their investigations. One of the tools they used were electromagnetic field (EMF) meters. EMF meters detect electrical and magnetic fields given out by electrically charged objects, and are often used to work out problems with electrical wiring. Ghost busters believe that changes to EMF may be associated with paranormal activity. However, stray radio frequencies can also make EMF meters go off. The team wanted to make sure their meters were measuring an intelligent response, and not merely background noise, so they announced that they'd leave the house they were investigating if they heard three short bursts of static – which they promptly received. They understood this to mean their presence was not welcome.

A digital recorder also seemed to capture an angrily hissing female voice. Was this a recording of a real ghost, perhaps the Red Lady? Or do our brains interpret sounds the way we want to hear them? This can certainly happen. It's possible to listen to a recording that sounds unintelligible, then when someone suggests that particular words are being spoken, we suddenly make them out and wonder why we didn't hear them before!

But what if the bursts of static and the voice on the recording really do reveal a ghostly presence? If the team did actually make contact with the ghost of a woman, who was she and why was she there? Was she really Mary Ann Lucas? Did she feel she had unfinished business? If you visit the island, you might find out. If you're brave enough, consider camping overnight, when most sightings take place. You can even go for a 'glamping' package, a glamorous form of camping, but be warned: that's not likely to impress the ghosts of hardened ex-cons!

A bolt from the blue

One of the main reasons Cockatoo Island was chosen to be a convict prison was its location. As with Alcatraz in San Francisco Bay, escape from the island was thought to be impossible. Indeed, many convicts tried to escape Cockatoo Island and died in the attempt.

But not Captain Thunderbolt. Although his name sounds like it should belong to an action hero, he was a real person. Born Frederick Ward in 1835, he was a drover who joined a horse-and-cattle stealing gang. Imprisoned on Cockatoo Island, he managed to escape along with another prisoner. How exactly they escaped isn't clear; there are conflicting stories. One version is that Ward hid in a boiler for four days. His loyal wife swam the shark-infested waters at night to provide him with food. Eventually he was able to make a break for it and he swam to freedom.

However he managed it, it's true that Ward went on to become one of Australia's most famous bushrangers. But how did he get his name? It wasn't because he bolted from gaol, though that would be fitting. Legend has it that Ward hammered loudly on a tollhouse door during one of his robberies. The tollhouse keeper complained about the loud noise, saying he'd thought it was a thunderbolt. Ward pointed his gun at the man, nodded at the gun and famously replied: 'I am the thunder and this is my bolt.' Nice!

OLD MELBOURNE GAOL

The things that happened in this brutal prison are enough to make you shout 'OMG' – which stands for Old Melbourne Gaol, of course. But did all that inhuman suffering lead to ghostly activity?

Grim reality of prison life

Victoria's oldest gaol imprisoned some of the colony's hardest criminals. But it wasn't only the rough and dangerous ones. Now a museum, the Old Melbourne Gaol also once housed people charged with minor crimes, such as petty theft, drunkenness and vagrancy (homelessness). Even the prisoners' children sometimes lived there!

Built in the mid-1800s, the grim bluestone structure stretches over three levels. People charged with the most serious crimes, such as murder or arson, would spend their sentence on the ground floor. For 23 gruelling hours a day, they would face solitary confinement in a tiny cell, with just a thin mattress to cover the hard slate floor. They were only allowed to bathe and change their clothes once a week – which isn't as much fun as it sounds! Think of the grimy sweat . . . the constant itching . . . the eye-watering smell – especially in summer. Those who broke the rules faced swift and brutal punishment.

Prisoners on the second floor had committed crimes that were considered a bit less serious, such as burglary or assault. They didn't fare much better. Men had to perform backbreaking labour and women had to clean, sew and cook under harsh conditions, often working around the clock in poor light until their bodies ached and their hands cramped and even bled. The third floor was for prisoners who had committed minor offences, such as petty theft or drunkenness. They had a marginally better stay, being given less arduous work and the chance to socialise with their fellow prisoners. Even so, the gaol was overcrowded, tough and unhygienic.

Ned Kelly's head

The gaol was closed in 1929, but not before 133 people were hanged there, including Ned Kelly, Australia's most famous bushranger. For the crime of killing a policeman, he was 'hanged by the neck until dead' in November 1880.

Like other executed prisoners, Ned Kelly's head was cut off and a death mask made. A death mask is a wax or plaster replica of a person's head, showing all their facial features and the contours of their shaved head. Immediately after death, a plaster cast was put on the prisoner's face and head. The cast was then used to make the physically accurate but completely creepy death mask. It sounds horrendous, but this wasn't done just to be grisly. Criminal researchers in those days believed in phrenology, a study which involved a close examination of the head. The idea was that criminal behaviour could be understood by studying facial features as well as the lumps and bumps on a person's skull. Have you ever heard the old saying not to trust a person whose eyes are too close together? That's a hangover from that way of thinking. Phrenology could be considered the precursor to modern psychology, but the newer science prefers to look inside a person's head, rather than outside.

Ned Kelly's death mask can be viewed in the museum today. But not his skull – it was stolen! It would be satisfying to think

the bushranger now haunts the old gaol, wailing and gibbering that he wants his head back . . . But no, there are no reports of Ned Kelly's ghost being spotted in the Old Melbourne Gaol. Pity! As for some of the other inmates? Well . . .

Cries of fear and anguish

The old gaol is reputedly haunted by the spirits of former prisoners. Visitors to the museum report an eerie feeling of fear and dread. Could it be that the prisoners' suffering was so intense it soaked right up into the prison's walls? But the reports go further than that. Particular cells are said to contain real live – or should that be real dead? – ghosts!

The Australian Ghost Hunters Society (AGHS) has made a study of the Old Melbourne Gaol. A non-profit organisation, their main motive is to try to uncover the truth. They note that cell 16 in the women's ward is the most famously haunted spot. Many visitors claim to have felt unnatural coldness in this cell, a sign often linked to ghostly activity. Perhaps spirits need to draw on thermal energy levels in order to manifest. Shadowy figures have also been seen lurking in the cell, and some visitors have felt so overwhelmed by negative emotions while in that cell that they couldn't bear to remain inside.

The AGHS report that a prior team of paranormal investigators had set up scientific measuring equipment in cell 16 in an attempt to capture objective evidence of ghostly activity. The team claimed to have made an EVP (Electronic Voice Phenomena) recording. The idea is that sounds which are inaudible to human ears may be picked up by digital recorders. The investigators were convinced that they captured the voice of an Irishwoman shouting furiously 'Get out!'. There's speculation the voice belonged to a

prisoner called Lucy. She died in cell 16, and her cry is said to be heard every year on the anniversary of her death.

The AGHS was also interested in another cell, known as the true condemned cell. This was where prisoners awaiting execution were held briefly before being hanged. The cell faces over the gallows and many people say the prisoners' intense emotions of terror and despair can still be felt. The investigators picked up on the emotions, but failed to receive readings on their equipment. Although they heard loud unexplained noises in some parts of the gaol, they concluded that the ghosts were not active that night, possibly due to the presence of too many people. Apparently, it's not unusual to get no result. Ghosts don't appear on demand!

Share your story

The AGHS points out that they don't have preconceived ideas about the paranormal. Rather, they are open-minded and think more evidence is needed to prove beyond doubt that ghosts exist. Members of the public are therefore invited to submit their own ghost stories and photographs. You can see them on the Castle of Spirits website: see 'Want more?' on page 137. Keep in mind that the AGHS doesn't vouch for the authenticity of these photos and stories in any way. They might be fake, they might be mistakes, or they might be real. Some of the photos are quite scary, so only look if you have a strong heart!

Great Scott!

Elizabeth Scott's claim to fame is one that no one would envy. In 1863, she became the first woman to be hanged in Victoria. When just 13 years old, Elizabeth's mother forced her into marriage with a much older man. Although shocking by today's standards, this was not uncommon back then. Life in colonial Victoria was harsh. Desperate men fled to the goldfields in the mid-19th century, often leaving their families behind to fend for themselves. Women in particular had difficulty making ends meet. Often unable to earn enough money to support themselves, they had to marry in order to survive.

The young Elizabeth and her husband Robert ran a bush inn, but their life together was far from content. Three of their five children died, and Robert was frequently drunk. The unhappy Elizabeth became friendly with two local men. One shot her husband and tried to make it look as if he had shot himself. Supposedly Elizabeth wasn't present when it happened, but that didn't save her from the law. Elizabeth and the two local men were convicted of murder and sentenced to hang.

Elizabeth Scott lived out her last days in Old Melbourne Gaol. Maybe that explains why her presence is felt there to this day, listlessly wandering the corridors, waiting for the reprieve that never came.

FREMANTLE LUNATIC ASYLUM

The living conditions in some psychiatric hospitals used to be as bad as those in prisons. Could severe overcrowding and vicious ill-treatment be behind the reported hauntings in an old Western Australian hospital?

You don't have to be mad to live here . . .

Even people we now consider sane were forced to endure life in the Fremantle Lunatic Asylum. Built in 1861, it was initially created to house 'lunatics' (an unkind term once used to describe people with psychiatric illnesses) in the Swan River Colony. Patients were a mix of both convicts and colonists. Treated as if they were hardened prisoners, patients had their heads shaved and were given second-hand prison uniforms to wear.

Some patients were indeed dangerous killers, but many were simply people in need of rest and protection. For example, the asylum housed people suffering from conditions such as depression, anxiety and epilepsy (where a person suffers from uncontrollable seizures, a condition that was poorly understood in the 19th century). It also contained people who, in those days, were considered 'morally insane' – people such as alcoholics and those who refused to work. Sadly, people who were unable to look after themselves and had no one to take them in were often also forced into the asylum as they had nowhere else to go. Dementia patients, deserted wives and the homeless were forced to live alongside criminals whose mental illnesses made them dangerous. There was no physical separation between the different types of patients, often leading to tragic consequences.

The death of one particular woman at the hands of a violent inmate sparked a public scandal. It led to a parliamentary enquiry, which found that patients at the asylum had been mistreated for decades. Straitjackets, isolation cells and floggings were all too common. The staff were not trained in the care of mentally ill patients. Some meant well, but not all. A matron was even accused of hitting patients with rods and keeping them awake by pricking them with hatpins!

Conditions were so appalling and chaotic, the asylum was compared to London's Bethlehem hospital, better known as Bedlam, which is the most notorious psychiatric hospital in history. The inquiry recommended the removal of all patients and the demolition of the rundown building. It took nearly ten years to move everyone to a more modern hospital, but the building wasn't knocked down as recommended. Rather, in 1909 it was turned into a poor house for destitute women: abandoned wives, unmarried mothers and the elderly. These poor souls fared no better than the psychiatric patients before them.

The Fremantle Lunatic Asylum is now a thriving arts centre
hosting music and arts events.

The building wasn't improved until 1942, when the women were removed to make way for a US naval base. It was quickly renovated to meet the high standards of cleanliness and hygiene demanded by the military. It seems the servicemen weren't quite as tough as the old ladies!

The building fell into disuse after World War II. At one stage it was condemned and scheduled for demolition. A push to restore historic buildings saved it from the bulldozers, however, and in the 1970s the asylum was turned into a museum and arts centre. Now known as the Fremantle Arts Centre, its traumatic history can be explored by history buffs and art lovers alike. The centre hosts art classes, exhibitions and live music events. But not all visits have been plain sailing . . .

Tales of the dead

Many people claim to have experienced unsettling hauntings when visiting the old asylum. Jane Hall, author of *May They Rest in Peace: The History and Ghosts of the Fremantle Lunatic Asylum*, described some of those harrowing experiences.

In her book, she states that one of the most commonly reported apparitions is that of an unhappy middle-aged woman. Clad in a black dress with a white frilled collar, she has been spotted wandering the grounds at night holding a lantern. There has been speculation that she was the ghost of a woman admitted in 1900. Her daughter had been abducted and the woman never

recovered from the trauma. Extreme mental anguish led to her being sent to the asylum and even while living as an inmate, she kept trying to find her child. Eventually the tortured woman fell from an upstairs window and died. Is it possible that she is still searching for her long-lost daughter?

Many visitors claim to have seen shadowy figures and heard disembodied footsteps. The sighting of nurses in coarse grey uniforms is not uncommon. Some visitors have even felt strong invisible hands pushing or touching them roughly. Perhaps there was so much suppressed fear and anger in the asylum, it's being echoed back today.

The art of haunting

According to Hall's book, artists and staff at the centre have been targeted by spirits. Cleaners have had dusters pulled out of their hands, and papers have been tossed around. A set of framed photographs was once found shattered, as if they had been hurled across the room. One artist was startled when his unfinished painting was violently thrown to the floor. Convinced a ghost

Is the ghost of a patient still
searching for her long-lost daughter?

didn't approve of his picture, he refused to finish it! Another artist had a harrowing experience when she heard her young daughter screaming. Rushing to her aid, the artist saw her daughter attempting to push away an unseen assailant. The little girl's plaits were standing upright, as if someone were pulling them.

But not all ghostly experiences have been negative. One worker, who was worried about her ill husband, felt gentle hands stroking her hair. She even received a kiss on the cheek! Might this have been one of the more caring workers in the asylum or poor house? Someone whose powerful desire to nurture the inmates lived on past his or her death? Whatever it was, it proves that it's not all bad!

A test of sanity

The concept of sanity was very different in colonial days. Anyone who acted in an unusual or socially unacceptable manner might have been considered not to be sane – even so-called 'rebellious' women who wouldn't do what their husbands told them to do! Some people with physical rather than mental disorders were also caught up in the system. Tourette syndrome, for instance, is characterised by involuntary sounds and movements, and it has been misunderstood for centuries. In medieval times it was sometimes seen as a sign of demonic possession. Nineteenth-century sufferers were considered insane. Modern medicine puts Tourette syndrome in its proper place, as a neurological condition.

So who would be considered 'insane' these days? Keep in mind that this is not actually a medical or psychiatric concept. It's a legal one, to be used as a defence in murder trials. The word 'insane' is now falling out of use in the law as it creates negative attitudes. In many parts of Australia the concept has been replaced with either 'mental impairment', 'mental illness' or 'mental incompetence'. Regardless of the terminology, the defence is used by people who are considered not responsible for their actions due to a medical condition.

Although laws vary between states, generally it has to be shown that at the time of the offence the accused was either unable to understand what they were doing, or that it was wrong. If successful, the jury verdict would be neither guilty nor not guilty, but rather not guilty by reason of their condition. Instead of being sent to prison, the defendant might be sent to a psychiatric hospital. The aim is to protect society from violence. But it is also to attempt to treat, rather than punish, the offender. Thankfully, dangerous patients are no longer kept alongside others requiring mental health treatment.

PRINCESS THEATRE

Melbourne's Princess Theatre is famous for more than its world-class performances. One performer is said to have loved the theatre so much that he refused to leave – even after his tragic death at the end of a show. The fact that he was playing the role of a demon is neither here nor there . . . or is it? Are the behind-the-scenes thrills caused by an actual ghost, or is it all just play-acting?

A dramatic death

The well-known landmark in Melbourne's theatre district was built in 1854. Although over 150 years old, the heritage-listed Princess Theatre is still being used for the performance of live plays, musicals and operas. It has been home to many block-buster productions including *Les Misérables*, *Cats* and *Hairspray*. In 1990 it became the first venue in Australia to host the perfor-mance of Andrew Lloyd Webber's musical *The Phantom of the*

This photograph of the Princess Theatre was taken in 1920. It looks much the same today, except it's now surrounded by skyscrapers.

Opera – which is quite fitting, really, considering that the Princess Theatre is rumoured to have a phantom of its own: a stage actor who died a rather dramatic death.

Back for the last bow

This is how it all started. The opera *Faust* opened at the Princess Theatre on 3 March 1888. The part of Mephistophcles, a demon, was played by Italian-born English actor Frederick Baker, who went under the stage name of Federici. Although only in his thirties, Federici suffered from a heart condition. The condition didn't stop him working, but the strain of rehearsals and the excitement of performing was finally too much for him.

The opera *Faust* traditionally ends on a dramatic note. The two main characters, Mephistopheles and Faust, appear to sink through the ground, as if descending directly into the pits of hell.

This is done by the clever use of a trapdoor on the stage, while a hidden choir sings a haunting chorus.

On that night, Federici and another actor stood on the trapdoor as it slowly sank downwards. By the time it reached the

Federici playing the demon Mephistopheles.

bottom, however, Federici had had a heart attack. He died almost immediately. The audience was completely unaware of this, as were most of the performers. Because, even though it's impossible, they all saw him return onto the stage, smiling and preening, taking the final bow!

The good-luck ghost

Since that night, the Princess Theatre has been said to be haunted by Federici. Staff and cast members over the years claim to have seen a solemn figure in evening dress walking up the aisles or across the stage. Reports of cold spots, shafts of light and the dusty smell of old lavender have also been made. Did Federici himself use this scent?

In 2004, the ABC documentary series *Rewind* did an episode about the theatre ghost. They spoke to Trina Dimovska, a cleaner who had felt an unmistakable touch on her hair and shoulders even though the theatre was closed and there was nobody there. Rob Guest, a theatre actor, also described his experience. One night he was playing the lead in *Les Misérables*. Standing backstage, he was preparing to go on to perform his scene. One of the ushers was certain she could see him in the dress circle, the first level seating platform. She was puzzled as to what he was doing there. Guest suspected it may have been Federici, all dressed up to play the lead role!

This was by no means the first time the ghost had been reported. In the early 1970s, a dramatised documentary was made in the theatre by Kennedy Miller productions. Nobody had noticed anything unusual, but a photograph of the film set startled everyone. When the picture was developed, it apparently revealed a pale, partly transparent figure watching the proceedings.

There's no suggestion that Federici is a malevolent ghost. Indeed, his presence has always been considered a sign of good luck. It's thought that if he appears, the stage show will do well. Federici's presence is so welcome, it became customary to keep a seat free for him in the dress circle. Sadly, this tradition had to end due to practical reasons. An empty seat means money lost. Some things are more frightening than ghosts!

A deal with the devil

Faust is a classic German legend. There are many different versions, but generally speaking the story is about a scholar who is frustrated by the slow progress of his studies. Faust encounters a representative of the devil, the demon Mephistopheles. They make a pact, and the demon agrees to serve Faust with his magical powers, giving Faust all that he desires in life. In return, the scholar's soul will belong to the devil.

Although at first Faust appears to be getting his heart's desire, things end up going horribly wrong. Faust wises up. He tries to repent and to reclaim his soul, but it's too late. Damned for eternity, the foolish man is carried off to hell by Mephistopheles.

THE QUARANTINE STATION

When people, animals or plants that have been exposed to infectious or contagious diseases enter a country, they need to be temporarily isolated, or placed in quarantine. The North Head Quarantine Station at Sydney saved many lives by stopping diseases from entering the community. Sadly, hundreds of people died there, their last days filled with fear and pain. Is that why the station is said to be haunted by tortured spirits?

Stopping epidemics

Located on Sydney's northern beaches, the old Quarantine Station is now a popular tourist centre, even containing a luxury hotel with scenic views over the harbour. But for most of its history, it wasn't exactly a desirable place to stay. Not that its residents had any choice in the matter!

Opening in the 1830s, the Quarantine Station was built to prevent unwell immigrants who had come to Australia on ships from entering Sydney. If even one person on the ship was sick, everybody on board had to be placed in quarantine until it was certain that they were well. Stays lasted 40 days on average. After that, healthy immigrants were allowed into the town to start their new lives.

All new arrivals had to enter the shower blocks for a disinfecting wash containing stinging carbolic acid. A few days later, the top layer of their skin would flake and peel off.

But not everyone was released. Until its closure in 1984, around 600 unfortunate people died at the station. They were isolated in the hospital ward, separated from family and friends for fear of spreading the virulent contamination. Patients died of frightening and debilitating diseases that included scarlet fever, smallpox, typhoid fever, cholera and the Spanish flu. Even the bubonic plague made its deadly appearance!

Be grateful for modern medicine!

In the station's early days, passengers were crowded into makeshift tents. Buildings were eventually constructed, but they proved to be inadequate. The site was hot, crowded, and unhygienic. Worst of all, the spread of disease was not properly understood back then. Many people who were initially disease free ended up seriously ill and even died of illnesses they contracted while they were at the station. For instance, healthy passengers were required to enter inhalation chambers, where they would breathe in steam infused with zinc sulphate. This chemical, known as white vitriol, was thought to offer protection from disease. The result was often the opposite. If an infected person had entered the chamber at the same time, the steamy conditions merely helped to spread the germs to the previously healthy people.

It wasn't until a smallpox epidemic swept through Sydney in 1881 – resulting in local residents being quarantined – that things began to change at the station. Complaints resulted in a Royal Commission and the station was improved. Also around that time, wealthy passengers began demanding better facilities. Class-based accommodation was introduced, with first-class passengers able to enjoy a higher standard of living. The stay became more pleasant for some, but not for everyone.

Despite improvements to the Quarantine Station, it struggled to deal with the 1918 to 1919 flu pandemic. Known as Spanish flu, this was one of the deadliest diseases in modern history. Coming hot on the heels of World War I, it killed more people than the war itself. About 500 million people – over one quarter of the world's population at the time – were infected. Up to 10 per cent of these people died, either from the disease itself or from complications. Shockingly, many of the victims were young and previously healthy. The severity of the outbreak was so bad that several of the nursing staff died at the Quarantine Station while trying to care for their patients.

Eventually medical breakthroughs, immunisation and improved quarantine processes meant that the station was no longer needed. In 1984, it became part of the Sydney Harbour National Park. Now a privately owned business, the station is known for its history and ghost tours. People aged 18 and over can even attend a paranormal investigation night, where they learn to use ghost hunting techniques and equipment. There are no guarantees as to what may or may not be found, however!

Ghosts at every turn

According to staff and visitors, the Quarantine Station is a hotbed of paranormal activity. Sightings purportedly include a nurse that patrols the hospital ward and a mortician dressed in a top hat. Apparently there's also a spirit that inspects people as they enter the inhalation chambers. If a visitor is sick, even with just a cold, the spirit becomes extremely distressed. When this happens, people on the tour have been so affected by the ghost's agitation that they've been known to vomit or faint.

Sydney's Quarantine Station has recently developed an international reputation. In 2010 it became the subject of the TV series *Ghost Hunters International.* In the show the investigators met up with the site coordinator, Caz Stokes, who described some of the astounding things she and others had experienced. These include the sighting of the ghost of a man in the shower stalls who was dressed as an attendant, where visitors have felt rough hands shoving them up against the wall. The coordinator herself claimed to have experienced bizarre activity in the hospital ward. She once heard snoring coming from an empty bed, and then in front of her eyes, the imprint of a person began to form on a mattress!

The shower blocks are said to be one of the many haunted places in the station.

The *Ghost Hunters International* team were led to the third-class dining area, which was built over an Indigenous burial site. Even so, the ghosts here seem to be related to the time when the area operated as the Quarantine Station. Said to be one of the most haunted spots on the site, a tour guide spoke of seeing a young boy crouched in a corner, sobbing inconsolably. On approaching him, the boy suddenly vanished. Even more disturbing are the stories of the kitchen, where a teenage girl in a pink dress has been known to stand near the dumb waiter, a small lift used for carrying food between floors in a building. She looks frail and harmless . . . until she starts wrapping her hands around people's necks. One visitor apparently ended up with red marks and bruising at her throat from this ghost!

The team carried out their investigation overnight. Members went to key areas, taking photographs and carrying out EVP recording sessions. They felt isolated temperature drops and heard disembodied noises, such as doors rattling and footsteps shuffling.

They detailed their startling analysis at the end of the show. A photograph taken just outside the hospital seems to show a shadowy figure standing near a fence. The team thought it looked like a young boy staring out at them through hollow eyes. The EVP recordings also had some astonishing results, recording what sounded like one of the investigators' names being spoken. And although they didn't hear it clearly at the time, a voice seemed to answer a question they asked while in the kitchen. They had asked how long the spirit had worked there. According to one interpretation, the quick-witted reply on the recording came back: 'Too long.'

A devastating disease

Smallpox was one of the worst diseases ever to strike humanity. Fortunately it is now considered eradicated, following a worldwide immunisation program led by the World Health Organization. In the past, though, it was the cause of many millions of deaths. It is estimated to have killed over 300 million people in the twentieth century alone. The disease has existed for thousands of years and it used to kill about one third of all the people infected. It was caused by exposure to a virus, which was spread easily and rapidly from person to person.

Smallpox was one of the diseases the Quarantine Station strived to keep out of Sydney. Tragically, this disease happened to be one of the biggest killers of local Indigenous communities in the early days of colonisation. Indigenous people hadn't been exposed to smallpox before, and so their immunity was much lower than that of Europeans. Some family groups were almost completely wiped out by the deadly disease. It's a tragedy there were no quarantine procedures around in those days to protect them from the diseases British settlers brought with them.

DUNTROON HOUSE

There are scarier things in Canberra than politicians! Duntroon House, part of Australia's military training facility, is reputedly haunted by a young woman who died under mysterious circumstances. Is her tortured spirit trying desperately to set the record straight and tell people how she died?

From mansion to mess

Built in 1833, Duntroon House is the oldest building in our nation's capital. It was built by Robert Campbell, a successful merchant. He was a descendant of the family that once lived in Duntrune Castle in Scotland, which is where the name came from. Duntroon House was passed down to Robert's son George, who developed and extended the property. It was their daughter – Sophia Susanna Campbell – who died a tragic and premature death there. But more about her later . . .

George and his wife, Marianne, spent several years in England, where their children were educated. After George's death in 1881, his widow and children returned to live at Duntroon. After Sophia's mysterious death a few years later, Marianne stayed on there until her own death in 1903. The house remained empty until 1910, when it was taken over by the Royal Military College. Duntroon House is now used as the officers' mess, or dining hall. But there seem to be things going on there that are curiously creepy!

Duntroon House is the oldest building in Canberra, built long before the creation of the Australian Capital Territory.

Messages from beyond the grave

In his book *A Case for Ghosts*, JG Montgomery examines the claims that Duntroon House is haunted. According to the author, witnesses have seen a young woman dressed in a long blue gown wandering around the property looking forlorn. Some people have glimpsed her in the gardens. Others have seen her pacing restlessly along the top floor of the mess, which used to be her home. There have also been reports that the bed in her old room at times appears to have been slept in, even when no one is staying there. At times windows and doors have closed by themselves, and the temperature has plummeted without apparent reason.

Montgomery also recounted something rather chilling experienced by Tim the Yowie Man, an author and seasoned investigator who runs ghost tours at various haunted sites, including Duntroon House. This might sound odd, but there is more to this anecdote than meets the eye. At the time of the writing of Montgomery's book, Tim had only ever had nose-bleeds twice in his life. Once was when he first entered the room where Sophia had died. The second was when he told a tour group that Sophia was believed to have fallen to her death. Was this just a coincidence? Or could it be something more? Could it be a message from the dead? Read on to see ...

Sophia's story

Sophia Susanna Campbell was born in 1857 and died aged only 27. There's a great deal of mystery surrounding her death. It's known that she fell from a first floor window – but nobody knows how or why she fell. Was it a freak accident? Did she jump? Or was she pushed?

According to the death certificate, Sophia died of apoplexy, or bleeding of the brain. It took her a whole day to die after the fall, during which time it's quite probable that she bled profusely from the nose. Does this make Tim the Yowie Man's nose-bleeds significant? Was Sophia's spirit trying to communicate with him in the only way she knew how? Perhaps she wanted to tell him that her death hadn't occurred in the way that he had suggested to the tour group. If this seems rather far-fetched, wait a little longer before you make up your mind: the coincidences don't end there.

Maree Agland is a researcher who has been published on the Hidden Canberra website. She too studied Sophia's death – and she too suffered from nosebleeds during her investigation. She said she underwent other bizarre experiences, including having strange flashes of falling out of windows and hitting the ground. She would smell grass and roses, then black out. Agland also claimed to have awoken one morning with torn ligaments and cartilage in both of her ankles and lower legs. The pain was so severe it felt as if she had fractured her lower right leg. These symptoms mimic what Sophia had suffered from her fall. Again, was this caused by Sophia's spirit trying desperately to communicate? Or perhaps there's an even darker explanation . . .

Could this all have been a threat? Agland's psychic friend believed that an evil entity had attached itself to her in an attempt to stop her researching Sophia's death. Indeed, the experiences stopped when Agland took a break from the work. Might this mean that Sophia had been murdered, and the murderer's spirit was trying to suppress the truth?

In her 2009 article 'Sophia Susanna Campbell – Duntroon, Canberra', Maree Agland recounted the many rumours surrounding Sophia's death. Some people believed that the young woman had become pregnant to the gardener, who rejected her. The rumours probably began because Sophia was buried next to a baby, but Agland noted that the grave in fact belonged to Sophia's little brother. Another rumour suggested Sophia was murdered by her father, who disapproved of the young woman's boyfriend. This is odd, seeing that her father died years before she did! Another opinion was that Sophia had an epileptic fit, causing her to fall from the window, and that the whole thing was a tragic accident. Yet another said she was trying to perform an acrobatic feat after visiting a circus, and that's how she fell.

A lack of evidence and the passing of time makes it unlikely that the truth will ever be known. People who believe in the paranormal, however, might see a significance in the fact that both investigators suffered nosebleeds. It may well have been an attempt by Sophia's spirit to communicate. More alarmingly, it might have been the spirit of a murderer trying to interfere with the investigation. Either way, this assumes that ghosts have the power to affect us physically and even inflict harm! Not a very comforting thought . . .

Keeping it in the family

As mentioned earlier, the Campbells were descended from the family that once owned Duntrune Castle in Argyll, Scotland. It's not just their residence Down Under that hosts a ghost. It appears that haunted houses run in the family!

Duntrune Castle was built in the 12th century and is one of the oldest continually occupied castles in the Scottish highlands. This 17th-century ghost story is set against the backdrop of tensions between different clans. The MacDonalds and the Campbells were at each other's throats. The MacDonalds wanted to seize the castle from the Campbells. Before trying to attack, they sent their piper over to spy on the Campbells. He was meant to assess how strong the castle was, and how good its defences were. The piper aroused suspicion and was captured. He played his bagpipes as a warning to the MacDonalds, but that was the last thing he ever did. His hands were ordered to be cut off and the unfortunate piper bled slowly to death.

This doesn't seem to be just a grisly story. During renovations in the 19th century, a handless skeleton was discovered beneath the basement floor of the castle. It appears the old story could be true, or at least based on truth. Maybe that explains the haunting bagpipe music that can sometimes be heard drifting through the cold night air. The piper might still be there, sending out his warning ...

PORT ARTHUR

There are so many haunted places in Tasmania's top tourist town that it's hard to pick which is the scariest. It might be the site where an old reverend lay splayed on the ground after tumbling out of his coffin. Or maybe it's the nanny's room, with the sturdy rocking chair that rocks on its own. Many people think the ghostly apparitions are connected to the town's convict past, but is there more than meets the eye?

A long and brutal history

This small and picturesque town is an open-air museum, a heritage-listed site containing many well-maintained buildings that date back to convict times. It sits on a peninsula about 60 kilometres from Hobart, Tasmania's capital. Although it started as a tiny timber station in 1830, Port Arthur is best known as one of Australia's most well-preserved penal colonies.

Due to its extreme isolation, the convicts brought to Port Arthur were among the most hardened of criminals. Often they were secondary offenders. Convicts were set to work carrying out backbreaking tasks, such as timber getting for the ever-hungry building industry.

From small beginnings, the desolate outpost grew rapidly. People who died while in the prison camps were buried on the chillingly named Isle of the Dead, an isolated burial ground without a chapel or church. But despite the hardships, the penal settlement was considered to be very advanced for its time. New ideas were starting to brew regarding the treatment of convicts. People were realising that the old-fashioned floggings and beatings merely turned prisoners into hardened criminals. It certainly didn't prepare them for life after imprisonment. Increasingly, it was seen that the better thing to do would be to equip prisoners with useful skills that would help them make a living after they were released. Prisoners were also rewarded for good behaviour, for instance with food or luxury items such as tea.

Despite these improvements, some things seemed to go downhill. The old-style corporal punishment was starting to be replaced with psychological punishment, which unfortunately wasn't much better! Rather than being whipped, prisoners were isolated for long periods, deprived of light and fresh air. The idea was that they would have time to reflect on their deeds – but for many it was emotional torture that led to irreversible mental illness. The fact that an asylum was built nearby says something about the way in which prisoners were treated.

The Port Arthur settlement began to dwindle in the 1860s and 1870s. No new convicts were being transported to Tasmania,

Port Arthur's old convict church was never consecrated.

and the existing ones were becoming too old to work. In 1877, the last convict was shipped out of Port Arthur, and it ceased to operate as a prison town. After the convicts left, a township sprang up among the old buildings. A conservation and development program helped it become a thriving tourist town, now managed by the Port Arthur Historic Site Management Authority. Much of the area's appeal lies in its historic and educational tours ... But don't forget the ghost tours!

Ghosts galore

Most people don't consider a visit to Port Arthur complete unless they join a ghost tour. In her book *Tasmanian Tales of the Supernatural,* Margaret Giordano described so many haunted places in the Port Arthur site, it's hard to pinpoint which is the scariest.

The ruins of the old convict church would have to be high on the list. Giordano explained that the church was the scene of great drama even when it was being built. While digging the foundations in 1835, one convict killed another by striking him brutally on the head with a pickaxe. The murderer was sentenced to hang. Many people think that's why the church was never consecrated – or declared a sacred place – but the reality is more mundane. It was never consecrated by any particular denomination because all the different religions worshipped there. They had to. There were no other churches in the settlement.

While the murder was grisly, there's nothing much mysterious about it. However, Giordano described an odd phenomenon related to the church. At one time, two convicts were quarrelling on the roof. One fell (or was pushed) to his death. Later, when the rest of the buildings lay abandoned and covered in ivy and moss, nothing would grow in the spot where the convict's blood had been spilled.

The parsonage next to the church is the scene of many reported hauntings. Giordano explained that when Reverend Eastman died there in the mid-19th century, his coffin couldn't be taken down the narrow stairs because he was so large! Instead, his coffin had to be lowered out of the window. One of the ropes broke under the great weight, however, and the poor man tumbled out of the coffin. People believe they have spotted him lying there on the ground to this day.

Witnesses have also seen eerie lights glowing in unoccupied rooms of the parsonage, and heard knocking sounds from no apparent source. When the building was being restored, a young labourer woke to feel a mysterious invisible weight pressing on his chest. After that, he refused to sleep on site again.

Strange lights glow from the church's bell tower and the bell has been heard to toll for no obvious reason.

And even more ghosts!

The commandant's residence also gets its share of ghosts. It's said to be haunted by the commandant himself, Captain Charles O'Hara Booth. The captain was the British officer in charge of the Port Arthur convict settlement. Apparently he stands at the window, dressed in his severe regimental uniform, as he looks out over the settlement. Keeping an eye on things, perhaps.

This building also houses an even creepier occupant. The nanny's room features a solid wooden rocking chair set in pride of place. It's a sturdy old chair, not given to easily moving in the breeze. Yet on several occasions it has been seen vigorously rocking all by itself, with no known physical explanation. It's said that the chair belonged to a nanny who didn't want to leave her job after a child she was looking after met with an accident. Is it possible that her spirit is still there, stubbornly refusing to leave?

A 20th-century tragedy

Port Arthur is also known as the scene of Australia's worst mass murder in modern times. It took place in 1996, but the painful events still feel fresh to the people who lost loved ones.

Thirty-five people were killed on that day, and more than 20 were injured. The shooter was sentenced to life in prison, never to be released. The events of that day so shocked the nation that new gun laws were introduced. They heavily restricted the availability of guns and high-powered weapons, in the hope of preventing something like this from ever happening again. Australia's gun laws have since become a model that other countries have tried to emulate.

WANT MORE?

For more information about these and other haunted places, have a look at:

- Australian Ghost Hunters website at http://www.castleof spirits.com/

- Giordano M, *Tasmanian Tales of the Supernatural,* Regal Publications, 2001

- Hall J, *May they Rest in Peace: The History and Ghosts of the Fremantle Lunatic Asylum,* Hesperian Press, 2013

- Heffernan J, *Haunted Australia,* Scholastic, 2005

- Miller J and Osborn G, *Something is Out There,* Allen & Unwin, 2010

- Montgomery J, *A Case for Ghosts,* Ginninderra Press, 2012

- Tim the Yowie Man, *Haunted and Mysterious Australia,* New Holland Publishers, 2006

UFO
SiGHTiNGS

You probably know that UFO stands for Unidentified Flying Object. This, however, doesn't mean much in itself. If something is labelled a UFO, all it means is that the object was flying and it hasn't been identified. It doesn't necessarily imply it's from outer space! Yet for many people, the acronym UFO is guaranteed to send a shiver down their spine. It conjures up images of pointy-chinned aliens with big eyes and even bigger laser guns. It feeds the suspicion that something is out there . . . and that it might not be something friendly!

There are hundreds, if not thousands, of reports of peculiar objects hurtling around the world each year. So what could these mysterious marvels be? They could be all sorts of things. They could be unfamiliar objects, or familiar things viewed from a strange angle, such as weather balloons, kites, aircraft or meteors. The sightings might even be optical illusions or the results of freak weather conditions. Or some might really be alien! We just don't know for sure.

Keep in mind that most UFO reports are fairly recent – from the early-to-mid-20th century onwards. Rather than being considered visitors from the stars, earlier sightings of strange lights or objects in the sky were sometimes put down to other things, such as ghosts, demons or omens from the gods. Take the example of Halley's Comet. This icy body hurtles through space, visiting Earth approximately every 75 years. It looks like a bright light with a streaming, sparkling tail. While many 20th-century witnesses interpreted the comet to be an alien spacecraft, in 1456 Pope Callixtus III declared it an agent of the devil!

Does this mean that aliens have only just started visiting us? Or perhaps they have been visiting us all along and we didn't realise it?

Some investigators believe aliens have been visiting Earth throughout our history. They even claim that ancient people had contact with aliens. This is because they suspect the ancients had access to technology that was beyond their time. For instance, that the pyramids of Egypt were built using complex technology that was far more advanced than what had been invented at the time – and that the technology therefore must have come from somewhere else. There's one flaw with this argument. It's problematic to underestimate the ingenuity of humans. People from the past weren't less intelligent than us. Just because a certain technology has been lost doesn't mean it never existed.

Believers in ancient aliens also point to unusual drawings and carvings that seem to be of aliens and/or spacecraft. A notable example is the Wandjina Petroglyphs (a group of rock carvings) in the Kimberley region of Western Australia. Dating back 5000 years, the petroglyphs portray figures with halo-like objects around their heads. Generally considered to depict spirits from the Dreaming, some commentators claim they are actually drawings of aliens wearing glowing helmets. This is all conjecture, however. We don't know what ancient people throughout the world had in mind when creating their artwork. Rather than imposing our world-view on the ancients, shouldn't we be taking ourselves back to their time and trying to see the world as they might have?

Anyway, that doesn't answer the question of why the number of UFO sightings has increased so significantly in more

recent years. Is it something to do with our culture? Technological changes influence our thoughts and beliefs. In less than a century, air travel has become commonplace. We've built magnificent telescopes, travelled to the moon and sent probes deep into the solar system. Not surprisingly, science-fiction stories and films have sprung up and gained popularity. It's possible that once the idea of aliens or space travel took hold, more people reported sightings. And then it had a snowball effect: these stories of sightings spread through the media, putting the idea into more people's heads, and then there were even more sightings. Maybe we humans are hardwired to come up with explanations that reflect our current culture.

Or possibly aliens really *are* coming now! Over the last century, we've been continually sending out radio signals. These signals leave Earth's atmosphere and travel into space. We've been drawing attention to ourselves lately! Maybe some curious aliens have decided to drop by and have a look.

However, the speed at which radio signals travel is far, far greater than the speed at which any of our human-made spacecrafts can travel. To arrive so soon after receiving our signals, the aliens' technology would have to be a lot more advanced than ours.

Maybe they *have* invented a far quicker way to cross interstellar space . . .

THE TULLY SAUCER NEST

In 1963, something – or someone – left a mysterious mark in the Horseshoe Lagoon in far north Queensland. What could have left the mark? And why?

The crop circle phenomenon

Crop circles first captured the public's imagination in the late 1970s and they've pretty much stayed there since. The idea that they are signs of extraterrestrial life was the subject of several television shows and films, such as the 2002 blockbuster sci-fi movie *Signs,* starring Mel Gibson.

A crop circle is a large shape, many metres across, that has been pressed into the vegetation of a field. Many patterns are so huge – hundreds of metres in diameter – that their design can only be viewed in full from the air. Although they're called crop circles, they aren't always circular in shape. All sorts of swirly patterns and geometric designs have appeared in crops. They can be complicated, and nearly always are beautiful. And they don't just show up in crops. As well as appearing in fields of corn and wheat, the patterns have been found imprinted into reeds and grasses.

Crop circles come in all manner of clever and beautiful designs.

A quick Google search will show how widespread crop circles are throughout the world. And Australia is no exception! In the last few years they have appeared in several places including a Northern Territory cattle station, in the Lachlan Valley near Yass, and in the Hunter Valley in New South Wales.

There's been a lot of debate as to what might create these shapes. Are they made by nature? Or are they marks left by UFOs? The simpler circles reportedly look as if they could have been the landing spots of spaceships. But what about the intricate, artistic patterns that started popping up all over the place from the late 1970s? Surely they can't be natural, can they? And surely it would be too much of a stretch to say they are landing marks of a spaceship ... The designs are signs of intelligence, hinting that the creators might have understood complex maths patterns such as fractals. Could it be that the creators were trying to tell us something, to communicate through the language of mathematics? Or maybe they were just showing off!

What caused the simple circles?

In his book, *The Secret History of Crop Circles*, Terry Wilson examines the theories about how simple crop circles are formed. One theory is known as the plasma vortex theory. It's pretty complicated, and involves electrified columns of air forming within whirlwinds. Under certain circumstances, the air gains a static charge that can flow down to the ground. This can leave a circular shape of flattened plants underneath it.

Another concept mentioned in the book was the orgone energy theory. Orgone is believed by some to be a type of energy associated with UFOs as well as other mystical phenomena. It's highly speculative and scientists don't believe this type of energy exists at all!

The author also speculated that the circles might be landing marks, or they might be coded messages from a higher intelligence. In some of the cases, witnesses claim to have seen the circles actually being made by strange objects.

This seems to be the story with the Tully Saucer Nest, which appeared in far north Queensland in the 1960s.

What happened at Tully?

On a clear summer's morning in January 1966, George Pedley was driving a tractor along a farm near the township of Tully. When Pedley approached Horseshoe Lagoon, he heard a peculiar hissing sound. He described it as sounding like air escaping from a tyre. But it was so loud, it could be heard over the tractor's noise.

Suddenly, an object rose out of the lagoon. Pedley said it was already about nine metres into the air when he first saw it. The object was large and grey and the shape of two saucers facing each other horizontally. Spinning rapidly, it rose another nine metres before taking off at a steep angle. Pedley drove to the spot and saw a large cleared area in the swamp grass. The water was churning slowly and seemed to be bare of reeds. He had another look a few hours later and saw that the bare patch in the lagoon had been replaced by a floating mass of broken reeds. They were swirling clockwise.

Burning with curiosity, Pedley told a friend and the property owner what he had seen. The men went to investigate and were astonished by what they saw. They waded into the mass and found that the reeds' roots had been ripped off the bottom of the lagoon. Later they found three large holes in the lagoon floor, lending weight to the idea that something

Maybe aliens have hobbies too!

had landed there. Something . . . alien? Neighbours later found other, smaller reed nests. Some of the pulled-up reeds in the nest rotated clockwise, some anticlockwise. Interestingly, they also found strange tracks nearby. What might have caused them, if the object could fly? Does this imply someone had been there, tampering with the reeds? Or could it mean something had come out of the object – perhaps to explore the area?

The news caused a media sensation. Many theories as to what caused the circles were flung around, the accused culprits including animals, whirlwinds and helicopters (as the blades of a hovering helicopter can blow reeds in a circular pattern). None of these theories were universally accepted, though. No known

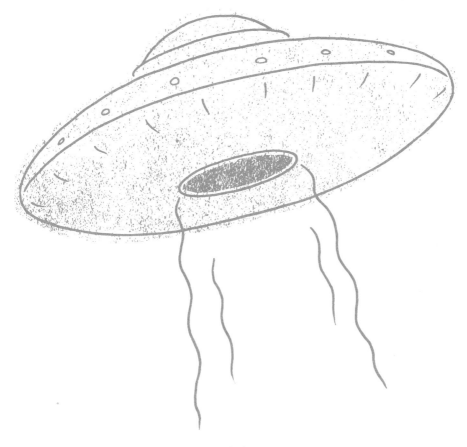

animals make nests like the one seen at Tully. And the weather was fine, which might exclude whirlwinds and vortexes. Helicopter blades only rotate in one direction, so it wouldn't explain why some circles twisted one way and some another.

Samples of the reeds were tested and there was no evidence that the reeds were burnt or exposed to radiation. What happened at Tully that day is still a mystery.

Crops and confessions

In 1991, two Englishmen made a confession. Doug Bower and Dave Chorley admitted that they had been making intricate crop circles, and were responsible for the first ones that appeared in Britain back in 1978. They even showed the world how they did it, inspiring others to copy them.

Many people have taken this confession to mean that *all* crop circles are hoaxes. But author Terry Wilson believes otherwise. He agrees that many of the intricate, post-1978 crop circles were probably man-made hoaxes. But he isn't so sure about the earlier, simple ones. Bower and Chorley actually claimed to have been inspired by these earlier ones – so who made those?

Making crop circles

Sorry, this isn't a how-to guide! Farmers don't like crop circles. They cause damage to their crops and cost them a lot of money. Going onto someone's field and making circles without permission is both trespassing and property destruction. Still, that hasn't stopped a proliferation of patterned plants appearing throughout the world.

Crop-circle makers are proud of their work. Many of them, including Bower and Chorley, consider it both a craft and a form of art. Some have gone to great lengths to show the world how it's done, performing demonstrations with ropes, posts and planks. They sometimes even get paid to go into someone's field and create these intricate designs. But remember: if you ever get the urge to crush innocent plants yourself, make sure you have the property owner's permission!

THE SEA FURY INCIDENT

Radars don't lie and they don't make mistakes . . . Or do they? How else can we explain the mysterious objects that buzzed around a Sea Fury aircraft back in 1954?

Caught on radar

The word 'radar' is an acronym for radio detection and ranging. A radar is used to detect the presence of objects by bouncing radio waves off them, then looking at the manner in which the waves are reflected back. Radar can work out how fast an object is moving and in which direction. It's used by the police to determine whether or not cars are speeding. It's also used to track aircraft, ships and weather formations. Without it we wouldn't have a modern aviation industry as the risk of planes colliding would be far too high.

It all sounds very scientific and reliable. And it usually is! But something odd happened on the night of 31 August 1954 that nobody can explain.

Lieutenant O'Farrell was flying a Sea Fury fighter aircraft on his way to the Royal Australian Navy Air Station in Nowra, New South Wales. At about 7.10 pm he saw a bright light approaching very quickly. It crossed in front of him and orbited around part of his aircraft. Soon afterwards a second, similar light joined the first. The stunned lieutenant had never seen anything like it before.

A Sea Fury aircraft, like the one piloted by Lieutenant O'Farrell in 1954.

He contacted the Nowra air station. Rather than immediately reporting his sighting, he asked whether any other aircraft were showing up on the radar. The radar operator confirmed that he could see two other craft on the screen, and asked who they were. O'Farrell didn't know. All he could see were vague shapes with white lights on top. But one thing was certain. Whoever – or whatever – they were, they shouldn't have been so close to him!

Eventually the lights sped off to the north-east. Intrigued by this mystery, the operator tracked them for a while, before losing sight of them from the radar screen.

When O'Farrell landed, he remained adamant as to what he had seen. His claims were so bizarre, he was checked thoroughly to make sure he hadn't been drinking or suffering from a medical condition. He was fine . . . but shaken and unable to understand what he'd witnessed.

The investigations

A secret investigation was performed by the military, but some of the information described above was somehow leaked to the media. The sighting and the information that was leaked sparked a great deal of public interest, but an official shroud of secrecy engulfed the matter for decades.

Nearly 20 years later, Lieutenant O'Farrell was interviewed by astronomer and ufologist Dr J Allen Hynek. Dr Hynek used to work for the United States Air Force. His role was to investigate whether various UFO sightings had astronomical explanations. For instance, were some unidentified flying objects actually meteorites? Dr Hynek had become so intrigued by his work with the air force that he started the independent CUFOS organisation – the Center for UFO Studies. He believed that UFO reports shouldn't be dismissed out of hand. Rather, they deserved serious scientific study.

After the in-depth interview with the lieutenant, Dr Hynek decided the Sea Fury incident couldn't be explained away by any known phenomena. In his opinion it was a genuine mystery.

Release of the files

The investigation was taken up by Australian Bill Chalker, the author of *The Oz Files: The Australian Story*. In 1982, Chalker requested the release of the official navy file on the incident, which had, until then, remained classified. Chalker's request was granted and he analysed the documents, including written statements by the pilot and the radar operator. He also took the opportunity to talk extensively with Lieutenant O'Farrell. The fact that so many years had passed might have eroded the lieutenant's memory to some extent, and this needs to be taken into account. Even so, Chalker noted that the lieutenant was a credible man. Rather than boasting about his experience, the pilot stressed that he'd wanted it all hushed up, as he had been afraid of looking like a fool.

Chalker was particularly interested in how the interview with Dr Hynek had come about. He learned that it had been set up through someone in a senior position at the Department of Defence. This suggests that interest in the case had reached the highest levels of government. The person who later became the Chief Defence Scientist had also taken a personal interest in the case.

What were the mysterious objects that swarmed around the lieutenant's plane?

Despite the investigations, both military and private, the case remains unsolved. No natural or earthly causes have been identified that could offer a rational explanation for what happened. The fact that the pilot's sightings were confirmed by radar means that he wasn't imagining it or making things up. *Something* was out there.

Some researchers believe the objects may have been the result of an unusual type of atmospheric disturbance. Another possibility is that they might have been space debris, for example, small meteors that vanished from the radar screens once they burnt up. This doesn't explain, though, why they were circling the pilot's aircraft. Others are convinced that the objects were alien scout ships, curious to learn more about our technology. To this day, nobody knows for sure what caused the radar blips – and the unidentified flying objects remain unidentified.

How reliable is radar?

Radar is considered to be very reliable, especially given recent advances in technology. Some planes, however, are designed to deliberately evade radar systems and radar-guided weapons. They are known as stealth aircraft and are used by the military.

But how can it be that a radar operator sometimes detects an object that no one else can see? This happened in Sydney in 1983. It caused quite a stir! According to news reports, senior radar operators at Mascot Airport detected unidentified objects flying north of Sydney. The objects were moving fast and appeared to be at high altitude. Nobody reported seeing the actual objects, but the radar images were undeniable.

The incident was taken seriously. Two **RAAF** (Royal Australian Air Force) fighter jets were placed on alert at the Williamtown base near Newcastle. They were ready to scramble and intercept the UFOs! Tests performed soon after showed that the blips were the result of radar interference, and not actual objects after all. Codenamed Operation Close Encounter, the fighter jets were never launched to head off the 'aliens'. But they came awfully close ...

THE WESTALL HIGH SCHOOL SIGHTING

In 1966, more than 200 witnesses believed they saw a UFO land before taking off again. Could such a large number of people all be mistaken?

An incredible sight

Most UFO sightings seem to take place in remote areas, late at night, with only one or two witnesses. But not this one. On 6 April 1966, an astonishing encounter took place in an ordinary Melbourne suburb, in the middle of the day – and was seen by hundreds! What's more, it wasn't just a fleeting glimpse of lights in the sky. The object actually landed. Some witnesses even claimed to have touched it.

The place was a field right next to Westall High School. The time: 11 am. Many of the students were out in the playground

and were shocked to see a flying saucer suddenly drop out of the sky.

Now adults, the memory of that frightening day has stayed with these witnesses. In 2010, several of the ex-students and teachers revealed what they had seen in a documentary screened on the Sci Fi channel. In the show *Westall 66: A Suburban UFO Mystery*, journalist Shane Ryan investigated the story behind the sightings.

Descriptions of the object varied somewhat, but that's to be expected after a gap of more than 40 years. Some people said they saw a silver disc, others described it as looking like a teacup turned upside down on a saucer. The unidentified object moved erratically. It hovered and darted and travelled at great speeds. Many witnesses claimed the object was accompanied by light aircraft that seemed to be tracking its movements. A few students ran to where the object appeared to have landed. When they got there, the object rose, sped off and vanished, leaving behind a circular patch of flattened yellow grass.

Was there a cover-up?

Students as well as other witnesses in the area reported seeing trucks and jeeps visit the site. They appeared to belong to the military, but the men's uniforms didn't match those of Australian forces. One witness claimed the uniforms matched those of the United States Air Force. Also, they arrived on the scene far too quickly – almost as if they were expecting something to happen.

The principal immediately called a school assembly. The students were told that the object was just an ordinary weather balloon. Then they were ordered not to discuss what they had seen with anybody. But if it was just a balloon, why the need for such secrecy? Why was a teacher's camera confiscated by a mysterious government official? And why was the grass at the landing site later cut and burned, destroying any visible evidence that something had recently landed there?

Evidence lost

Despite warnings not to talk to the media, one student did just that. The story was aired by Channel 9 not long after the incident. But when journalist Shane Ryan tried to find the original television footage from 1966 for the 2010 documentary *Westall 66*, he learned that it had disappeared. Had some anonymous official forced Channel 9 to surrender the tapes after they had been aired? Had they been destroyed or taped over? Or were they accidentally misplaced? All the primary evidence that now remains is a report in the *Dandenong Journal*.

So. What might the strange object have been? A UFO? A mass hallucination? Secret military equipment? Given the timing and the official government reaction, military testing seems the most likely. But what do you think?

The front page of the Melbourne newspaper the *Dandenong Journal* dated 14 April 1966.

The space-obsessed sixties

UFO sightings appear to have been at an all-time high in the 1960s. Perhaps that's not too surprising considering the Cold War reached its frightening peak in the same decade. The Cold War between the United States and the Soviet Union was characterised by a continual state of tension and hostility between the two superpowers. Each tried to outdo the other in technological advances, the competition spurring them on to demonstrate their superiority. Part of the Cold War was the Space Race. Who could put a man on the moon first: America or the Soviet Union?

With the focus firmly on space, the concept of space travel and alien life took a hold on the world's imagination. Television shows such as *Doctor Who* and *Star Trek* sprang up during the 1960s – and indeed are still popular today. With all this focus on space, could some of the UFO sightings in the 60s have actually been sightings of secret weapons or surveillance technologies?

Government secrets

The curious thing about UFO sightings is that when the official government position is that nothing happened, it makes people question their government. Is important information being kept from us? If so, why?

The world is rife with UFO-conspiracy theories, the most famous involving the Roswell incident in the United States. In July 1947, an unidentified object is said to have crash-landed following a severe thunderstorm. A worker on a ranch in the state of New Mexico discovered piles of debris spread across a large area. The wreckage consisted of metal, rubber and bits of wood. The Roswell Army Air Field spokesperson initially stated that a flying disc had crashed, but the official story changed after the government scientists turned up. They claimed it was merely an ordinary weather balloon.

A few decades later, the story hit the headlines in a big way, capturing the imagination of the world. That was because someone came forward and claimed that in 1947 the government had carried out autopsies (medical examinations of dead bodies) on three aliens. Video footage of the autopsies was uncovered, and has since been screened on numerous documentaries.

Today, most experts believe the footage was a hoax. Even so, the incident fuelled rumours that aliens really had landed in July 1947 in New Mexico and the government deliberately hid the truth.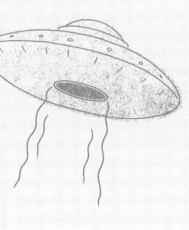

Maybe we're not always told everything. It's been made clear in recent times that governments like to keep their secrets. But that doesn't mean they're hiding information about aliens.

Slowly, the truth may eventually come out. Or it might not ...

THE VALENTICH DISAPPEARANCE

Pilot Frederick Valentich made a chilling statement over his aircraft's radio before disappearing forever. Did a strange object really chase him across the sky, and could it have been an alien ship?

An astonishing conversation

At 6.20 pm on 21 October 1978, 20-year-old Frederick Valentich took off from Melbourne's Moorabbin Airport. He was heading towards King Island in Bass Strait, supposedly to pick up an order of crayfish. Valentich was a licensed pilot with a reasonable amount of flying experience. Conditions were good and visibility was clear. The single-engine Cessna 182 he was flying had recently been serviced and everything should have gone smoothly. Yet something strange happened – something that continues to fuel speculation to this day.

According to Air Traffic Control in Melbourne, Valentich made a standard position report while flying over Cape Otway, at the bottom of mainland Australia. Then, nearly 50 minutes into the flight, he contacted control again. This time, the stress in his voice was clear. The transcript of the conversation was later released by the Australian Department of Transport. Reading it gives you goosebumps!

A chilling conversation

Valentich asked whether there was any known air traffic in his area flying below an altitude of 1500 metres. Air Traffic Control replied that there wasn't. The pilot, however, claimed that a large aircraft was flying near him. Sporting four bright lights, which he thought were landing lights, the mysterious object had passed over his aircraft a few times and orbited around him. At times it appeared to vanish. Valentich thought it was playing some sort of game. When asked to describe the object, he said it was long, shiny and metallic, with a bright green light.

Valentich also reported that his engine was rough idling, meaning it was in trouble. His conversation with Air Traffic Control lasted about six minutes and, right at the end, Valentich said the object was near him yet again. His final spine-tingling words? 'It is hovering and it's not an aircraft.' After that, all that could be heard was a series of strange metallic scraping sounds . . . then nothing. The line went dead.

Nothing more was heard from Frederick Valentich. There was no evidence of a crash, and his aircraft has never been recovered. What might have happened to him?

A human tragedy or an alien abduction?

If you've read about the Bass Strait Triangle (page 78) you'll know of the mysterious disappearances of ships and planes that have taken place there for over a century. It'll come as no surprise, then, that Frederick Valentich was flying through the triangle when he vanished. In fact, his disappearance contributed to the nicknaming of this part of the strait as the Bass Strait Triangle, after the infamous Bermuda Triangle, which lies off the coast of the United States.

This tragic disappearance of a young man sparked many theories as to what may have happened. Some people think it was a simple matter of human error and/or engine failure. Valentich might have become disorientated in the darkening skies, even to the point of flying upside down. The lights he had seen may have been his own aircraft's lights reflected in the ocean. But is this physically possible?

In 2013, the Discovery Channel aired an episode of *The Unexplained Files* that explored the Valentich disappearance. George Simpson, who was interviewed on the show, believes himself to be one of the last people to have seen the plane in the air. Simpson was standing outside his house at around 6 pm, waiting for his girlfriend to arrive for dinner. He happened to notice a Cessna flying over. Judging by the angle, he believed the plane was flying directly to Cape Otway. Simpson later learned about the disappearance of the plane and pilot, and he developed such an interest in the story that he investigated it thoroughly.

Simpson met with a Cessna expert to see whether the flying-upside-down story was feasible. The expert believed that the Cessna's fuel tank wouldn't be able to run upside down. The

Were the lights that Frederick Valentich described his own aircraft's lights reflected in the water?

engine would quickly stop and he estimated that the plane would fall within approximately three minutes. The pilot's conversation with Air Traffic Control lasted twice this length of time, meaning the expert believed Valentich was not flying upside down that long.

Another theory was that Valentich had made the whole thing up so that he could disappear without a trace. Perhaps he had a reason for wanting people to believe he had died, or maybe he had even gone so far as to take his own life. On the show, a flight service officer flagged this as a possibility, based on his concerns over the haphazard nature of Valentich's flight plans. The flight service officer pointed to the fact that Valentich hadn't pre-ordered the crayfish he was meant to pick up, nor had he contacted anyone at King Island airport to let them know he wanted the runway lights switched on.

THE UNKNOWN

This plaque commemorates the landmark of the mysterious disappearance of FREDERICK VALENTICH on 21 October 1978.

Frederick was flying a Cessna 182L, and at this point he changed direction to south from the lighthouse towards the sea.

Twelve minutes flying south from here at precisely 19:12:28 hrs radio transmission was cut off and in his last radio contact he explained "that strange aircraft is hovering on top of me again, and it is not an aircraft......"

After an extensive land and sea search, no trace was ever found of the Cessna VH-DSJ or of FREDERICK VALENTICH.

And so to this day, his disappearance remains a mystery.

This memorial plaque was erected by the Valentich family at Cape Otway, Victoria, in memory of their loved one who vanished without a trace.

Valentich's family didn't believe this suggestion, however. They said that he wasn't depressed, nor was he likely to play cruel games with people and disappear on purpose. He may have been a UFO buff, but that didn't mean he would go to such extremes – such as making up a sighting and staging an abduction – to prove a point.

Furthermore, these theories can't explain the fact that other people have come forward saying that they too saw strange lights in the sky that night.

The question remains: did Frederick Valentich encounter an unidentified object hovering next to him in the sky? If he did, what was it? And why was he never seen again?

He wasn't the only one!

Frederick Valentich isn't the only pilot to have reported strange things in the sky. Known as UAP, unidentified aerial phenomena refers to unusual lights or objects that are encountered by aviation professionals while an aeroplane is flying. There have been literally thousands of sightings of UAP throughout the world, made by pilots, air crew, radar operators and air traffic controllers.

The American non-profit research group NARCAP – National Aviation Reporting Center on Anomalous Phenomena – was set up to analyse these encounters. It was founded by scientist Dr Richard Haines, who has also written a book about the Valentich disappearance. Haines believes that UAPs may pose a real threat to aviation safety. Might they be the cause of some air-related accidents and near misses? He calls on aviation professionals to share their experiences on the organisation's website so that they can be studied and properly analysed.

ENCOUNTER ON THE NULLARBOR PLAIN

While driving across the Nullarbor Plain, an ordinary family faced an extraordinary situation that scared them half to death. Could they really have had a close encounter with a UFO?

A shocking sight

In January 1988, the Knowles family and their dogs set off on a long road trip from Perth to Melbourne. Mother Faye and her three adult sons shared the driving, which is a completely normal thing for families to do. But they also shared an experience that was anything but normal! It happened a little before 5 am on 20 January. The family was travelling across the Nullarbor Plain in an area called The Basin, in Western Australia.

Twenty-one-year-old Sean was driving, and everyone was awake. Sean saw a bright light approaching. At first he thought

The Nullarbor Plain is flat, semi-arid and feels endless. It's located between the Great Australian Bight and the Great Victoria Desert.

it was the headlight of a truck, but the light jumped around in a very un-truck-like manner. The light grew larger, disappeared, then reappeared behind them.

The family described the bizarre object as being bright white with a yellow centre. The shape was like an egg in an eggcup. It was only about one metre wide – not wide enough to be what we'd consider an aircraft, but wide enough to block the road.

The sequence of events that followed is not exactly clear, and some of the reports are garbled. At times, different members of the family said different things, but that's not surprising given the amount of stress they were all under. It seems agreed, however, that Sean had to swerve into the oncoming traffic lane to avoid hitting the object.

Chased by a UFO

The family drove past the object, then curiosity got the better of them. They stopped, got out of the car, and went back to take a closer look. Something frightened them, though, and they ran back to their car and drove away. But the object gave chase! At one point Sean was driving at 200 kilometres per hour in an attempt to escape. It seems to have been during this time that they felt something thud onto the roof. Faye Knowles reached a hand out of the window and touched the object. It felt hot and spongey. Shocked, she brought her hand back inside the car. It was covered with a fine black dust. A smoky mist started to fill the car. Foul-smelling, it sent them into a panic.

It was about then that things became even more bizarre. The family reported they felt the car being lifted into the air. While the car was floating, their voices became distorted and sounded like they were speaking in slow motion. One of the sons reported feeling like his brain was being pulled from his head.

The car dropped violently to the ground and the impact caused a tyre to blow. Fearing for their lives, the Knowles family ran from the vehicle and hid in a bush. When they felt certain that the mysterious object had gone, they changed the damaged tyre. The car was covered in soot and there were four dents in the roof, as if something had landed on top.

The Knowles family drove 600 kilometres to the Ceduna police station, where they reported the incident. For some unknown reason, they passed the much-closer police station at Eucla. Perhaps it took time for them to calm down and evaluate the situation before deciding to report it. According to the policeman who took their statement at Ceduna, the family were genuinely distressed, which makes it seem unlikely that it was all a hoax. They seemed convinced they had encountered a UFO.

Samples were taken from the car for scientific testing. The policeman also suggested the family contact ufologists in Adelaide and he set up a meeting for them.

Is it possible that the Knowles family really did encounter a UFO? Or might there be another, more earthly explanation?

Queries and theories

The first question to ask was: did anybody else see the strange object? And the answer is yes! A truck driver who was ahead of them on the road reported seeing a light above the Knowles' car in his rear vision mirror. He said it was hovering above the sweeping stretch of road, flickering in and out between the trees. When he later met up with the family at a motor hotel, he found them in a state of shock. Even the dogs were cowering in fear. The truck driver also reported that the family's car had an odd smell. He said the car smelt like bakelite (an old type of plastic) or as if they'd blown a fuse.

It seems clear that the Knowles family did experience *something* that day. But what could that something be? The magazine *Skeptic*, which explores paranormal claims, examined the matter. In a 1988 issue, the magazine described the results of the car's scientific testing. The lab that carried out the tests said the dust on the car was material from burning shredded rubber and from brake linings. This was most likely due to Sean

Knowles braking at high speed and from the tyre blowing out. The lab also claimed the dents on the roof were not fresh and that they were made at an earlier time, perhaps by something as ordinary as a roof rack.

The magazine looked at the theories put forward both by sceptic groups and by ufologists. Some of the ufologists urged caution and wanted more details about what had happened before coming to a conclusion. Others were convinced the Knowles family had encountered an extraterrestrial research vehicle sent down by its mother ship to do scientific tests on Earth. One commentator even wondered whether the family might have been abducted and then had their memories wiped before they were returned!

As for the sceptics mentioned in the article, one suggestion was that the Knowles family had seen an optical illusion caused by the bending of light rays. The light source might have been an oncoming vehicle or the rising sun. Glen Moore, a physics lecturer at the University of Wollongong, raised another possibility. He suggested that a meteorite had fallen and disintegrated, which would explain the smell and the glowing light. Professor Peter Schwerdttergger, head of meteorology at Flinders University, thought the whole thing might be the result of a dry thunder-storm – a storm with lightning but no rain – which would explain why the car shook violently.

The problem with the scientific explanations put forward is that no single theory can explain everything the Knowles family claimed took place. It seems that something frightening and extraordinary happened to the Knowles family early that morning – so extraordinary that nobody can explain it.

Close encounters of the what kind?

The term 'close encounter' was originally coined by Dr J Allen Hynek, an astronomer and UFO expert, in his book *The UFO Experience: A Scientific Inquiry*. The term became well-known after the success of the 1977 sci-fi film *Close Encounters of the Third Kind*. But what are the different types of encounters, and what do they mean?

According to Hynek, a close encounter of the first kind refers to a sighting of a UFO from a distance of 150 metres or less. A close encounter of the second kind refers to a sighting accompanied by physical effects such as heat or electrical interference. The Knowles family's experience would come under this category. So what about the third kind? That's when there's a sighting of an actual alien!

Other UFO experts have since added extra categories. A close encounter of the fourth kind refers to abduction cases, where people are taken by aliens, generally against their will. These experts believe aliens take humans for the purposes of study, so they can learn more about us and about the Earth. Has anything like that ever happened in Australia? Read on and see . . .

THE KELLY CAHILL ABDUCTION

When people who claim to have encountered UFOs are unable to account for lost time, the question often arises: is there a possibility they were abducted by aliens?

Taken for testing

Alien abduction stories follow a typical pattern. They usually begin with the sighting of an unidentified object, and are followed by physical symptoms such as dizziness or nausea. The witness then passes out or loses consciousness. When they recover, a significant amount of time has passed and they can't explain why. Often the witnesses don't immediately have memories of strange events, but later on things start to come back to them. Maybe in dreams. Maybe under hypnosis. Maybe it just hits them. They start to recall meeting aliens. They might remember uncomfortable or even painful medical examinations being performed on them. And with the memories comes fear.

This was the case with one of Australia's most famous UFO abduction stories. In August 1993, Kelly Cahill and her family were driving through an outer Melbourne suburb near the Dandenong foothills. It was around midnight, and they were returning home from a party. Suddenly they saw a bright light ahead. They kept driving, turned around a bend in the road, and saw a house-sized craft sitting in the middle of a field alongside the road. Although stunned, Kelly's husband decided to keep driving – and that was the last thing they remembered. For the time being, at least.

The Cahills drove back home. Kelly's heart was pumping like mad and she could smell vomit. Time seemed to have passed that they couldn't account for. That night, Kelly suffered from severe abdominal pain and was eventually hospitalised with an infection. A weird mark was found below her belly button, like a burn but without any blistering. It was in the shape of a perfect triangle, and she had no idea how it had gotten there.

To top it all, Kelly was plagued by strange dreams related to UFOs and aliens.

A few weeks later, when the Cahills were driving along the same stretch of road, memories of what happened that night suddenly returned.

The memories return

Although Kelly's recollections were confused and fragmented, she was convinced that she could remember getting out of the car with her husband and walking towards the UFO in the field. As they walked, they reportedly encountered a tall black figure with burning red eyes. Other similar beings also approached them.

Kelly Cahill describes her extraorinary experiences in her book, *Encounter*.

Terrified, Kelly somehow sensed that they were evil. She suddenly started shouting that they had no souls. On reflection, she couldn't explain how she could have known this, but it might have been connected to the spiritual quest she had been undertaking at that time in her life. She also remembered shouting that the beings were going to kill them. Perhaps as a punishment or as a warning to keep quiet, she was hit hard in the stomach. Kelly flew through the air, landed on her back and fought hard not to lose consciousness. Kelly recalled hearing her husband arguing with the beings. An alien insisted they didn't mean any harm and that they were peaceful. Her husband challenged that, asking them why they had hit his wife. Kelly didn't believe their assertions either. Hysterical, she started screaming

Who – or what – were the strange beings that Kelly Cahill believes she encountered?

that they could not be trusted. She felt violently nauseated and she thinks she must have blacked out for a while. The next thing she knew, she was sitting back in her car, feeling shaken and smelling vomit.

Can anyone confirm Kelly Cahill's story?

The incredible thing about this story is that it appears to be confirmed by independent witnesses! It has been claimed that other people were present and were also caught up in the strange events.

The story was explored on the television show *The Extraordinary,* an Australian series that investigated paranormal events. Apparently two other cars were on the scene. The driver of one of the cars never came forward and was never identified. The people

in the other car, married couple Jane and Bill and their friend Glenda, refused to come forward publicly or talk on the show. We don't even know their full names. However, they supposedly gave an account of their experience to UFO investigator John Auchettl of Phenomena Research Australia (PRA), who was interviewed on the show.

Auchettl said that Jane and Glenda also saw the aliens but, unlike Kelly Cahill, they were not frightened. The women believed they had been transported from the field into the UFO. They too awoke with strange markings on their bodies. Their descriptions and reports were startlingly similar to Kelly's. For some reason, however, the men – Jane's husband and Kelly's husband – didn't appear to have had these experiences.

Auchettl also claimed to have taken soil samples from the place where the UFO had supposedly sat. Laboratory tests he had conducted showed that there had been changes in the soil chemistry. There was an above average sulphur content, as well as traces of an uncommon carbon compound called pyrene. He also said there was a triangular-shaped patch of dead grass on the site.

If it were only Kelly Cahill making the abduction claim, it would be tempting to think she may have been mistaken. Perhaps she had been under a lot of stress, or maybe she confused a dream with reality. The independent evidence, however, seems to make her story much more feasible.

But can it be relied upon? Did these extra witnesses even exist? Unfortunately Auchettl's report has not been released so it's hard to say! It's difficult to accept someone's word, especially when their claims are so extraordinary. If proof exists, why would it not have been made available to the public?

Is it possible to have false memories?

False memories are memories that feel real even though they never happened. It sounds unbelievable but unfortunately human memory is not particularly reliable. It isn't the same as a video recording that we can replay whenever we feel like it!

You've probably heard people arguing over something they both experienced happening, disagreeing over details big and small. Both insist that they are right – after all, they remember! But everyone has their own memory of an event, and memories change with time. They fade, and they can even become distorted or contaminated.

Many people who claim to have been abducted by aliens do not seem to be lying. It's likely that some are hoaxes, of course, but other abductees seem passionate and genuine. But does believing something happened necessarily mean that it did happen? Did these 'abductees' actually experience what they claim?

There's a very real possibility that some of these people are experiencing false memories. Psychologist Elizabeth Loftus is an expert on the reliability of memory. She has demonstrated on countless occasions how flawed people's recall can be.

One experiment was performed on a group of people who had all been to Disneyland when they were children. Some were encouraged to associate Bugs Bunny with the experience. They were later asked whether they remembered meeting the giant rabbit at Disneyland and shaking his hand. Many of them agreed they could indeed remember this. Some even added more details related to the meeting. 'So what?', you ask. 'Maybe they really did meet him!' Except ... They couldn't have. Bugs Bunny has nothing to do with Disney. He's a Warner Brothers character who wouldn't be seen dead at Disneyland!

It seems that false memories can be created if they are planted or encouraged by an authority figure. Being asked to imagine an event makes it more likely that it will start to feel like a real memory. Having someone else pretend to confirm an event also increases the chance of a false memory developing. It sounds odd, but it happens all the time. Let's see ... Do you really remember the time you were lost in the mall when you were three? Or do you just remember your mum telling you about it?

WANT MORE?

For more information about these and other mysterious un-identified flying objects, see:

- Cahill K, *Encounter,* HarperCollins, 1997

- Chalker B, *The Oz Files: The Australian UFO Story,* Duffy and Snellgrove, 1996

- Gilroy R & H, *Australian UFOs: Through the Window of Time,* URU Publications, 2004

- Haines R, *Melbourne Episode: Case Study of a Missing Pilot,* Lighting Design Association, 1987

- Wilson T, *The Secret History of Crop Circles: Recording the Phenomenon in Days of Old,* The Centre for Crop Circle Studies, 2015, and his website http://oldcropcircles.weebly.com/

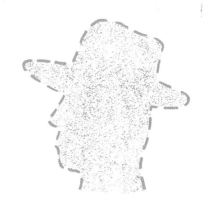

BiZARRE
DiSAPPEARANCES

People can disappear for many reasons. They might fall victim to an accident, become ill or lose their memory. They might become disoriented and not be able to find their way home. Some people actually decide to disappear, having all sorts of reasons for wanting to vanish and quietly start a new life. Sadly some people meet with foul play – but unsolved crimes aren't the subject of this book. We're interested in things that are less grisly and more spooky!

It's not just individual people who disappear. Groups, ships' crews, and even hundreds of passengers have been known to mysteriously and tragically vanish without trace. In the past it was relatively easy for this to happen, particularly in isolated places and particularly in Australia. It is so big that you could

fit all of Europe inside, yet it's still full of vast uninhabited areas. Maybe we shouldn't be so surprised when things go missing in this big beautiful country of ours . . .

But modern technology, such as telecommunications and GPS (global positioning system), has given us new ways of keeping tabs on people. So when someone or something genuinely goes missing these days, it can cause quite a stir.

Naturally, bizarre disappearances are surrounded by all sorts of rumours. Was it pirates? Ghosts? Aliens? Holes in the fabric of time and space? Read on and see!

THE LOSS OF LUDWIG LEICHHARDT

Ludwig Leichhardt was a German-born explorer. His disappearance – along with six other men, seven horses, 20 mules, 50 bullocks and loads of equipment – is one of the most famous in Australian history. How could such a large expedition vanish without trace?

A good track record

There are several places called Leichhardt in Australia, including suburbs, rivers and roads. You might know of some of them. We tend not to give place names much thought, but often there's an interesting story behind the name. That's certainly the case here. This is a story of courage, curiosity and determination that sadly ended in lives lost.

Friedrich Wilhelm Ludwig Leichhardt was born in 1813 in Trebatsch, Prussia, now Germany. He had a passion for botany and the natural sciences and a burning desire to explore Australia's vast interior. At that time, European settlers had no idea what was in the middle of Australia. They didn't know whether it was lush or harsh, inhabited or empty. The government wanted to encourage expeditions into the unknown and even offered grants to explorers. Leichhardt had poor eyesight and no bush skills, but that didn't stop him pursuing his dream.

In 1844 he led his first expedition in Australia. Starting at the Darling Downs in Queensland, he led his team west then north, eventually ending at Port Essington in the Northern Territory. Throughout the journey food was in short supply and the

Leichhardt's first successful expedition opened up vast areas of inhabitable land that were previously unknown to Europeans.

team was in danger of starvation. They were gone so long, they were presumed to be lost. Fortunately they learned to live off the land and most of them managed to survive the ordeal. The team returned triumphant, with tales of having discovered new lands. Leichhardt also proved himself an able botanist, having catalogued thousands of specimens of native plants and animals.

The expedition was a success and the team were greeted as heroes. Leichhardt gained fame as a daring scientist and explorer and was awarded gold medals from both the London and Paris geographical societies. But his taste for knowledge and adventure was still not satisfied. If anything, his ambitions grew larger. Leichhardt wanted to cross Australia from east to west, right through the mysterious centre. His first attempt ended swiftly due to poor weather and illness. But in April 1848 he set out again, determined to succeed this time. Sadly, the expedition was a failure. The large team, complete with masses of equipment, was never seen again.

How far did they get? And what caused them to vanish? Nobody knows, but that's not for lack of trying!

How could such a large expedition vanish without a trace?

Lost in the outback

Several expeditions have set out to look for Leichhardt's remains, and the search continues even to this day. Numerous books and reports have been published about the subject. Even the acclaimed novel *Voss*, by Australian author Patrick White, was inspired by Ludwig Leichhardt.

One of the most puzzling aspects of this mystery is what happened to all the equipment. As well as dozens of animals, Leichhardt's team set off with pots, plates, axes, saddles, horseshoes and so on. How can it be that absolutely none of these durable items have been recovered?

There may be a shortage of relics, but there's no shortage of rumours. Some people believe the expedition members were killed by Indigenous people, perhaps because Leichardt and his group trespassed on sacred places. Others think there may have been a mutiny, or that the group died of starvation. Still others believe the party drowned while trying to cross a river, which may explain why the equipment has never been found.

Sifting through the evidence

Dr Darrell Lewis is an archaeologist, historian and bushman. Working in the outback for more than 40 years gave him the skills needed to help solve the mystery. In his book *Where is Dr Leichhardt? The Greatest Mystery in Australian History*, he examined the clues and analysed the evidence, trying to find the route that Leichhardt's expedition took.

There wasn't a lot to go on. A few trees had been found with the letter L carved on them. Stories of contact with Europeans were passed down through generations of Indigenous people. But by far the best evidence was a brass nameplate from a rifle with 'Ludwig Leichhardt' written on it.

According to the story, the plate was found in 1900 in a boab tree, attached to a disintegrating gun. The tree even had a letter L carved on it! Unfortunately its exact location is no longer known. The plate was found by an Indigenous man, who gave it to his boss. After changing hands it finally ended up in Canberra's National Museum of Australia.

The discovery of the plate hasn't solved all the mysteries related to Leichhardt's expedition. It doesn't tell us where he died or how far he got. But it does suggest he made it at least two-thirds of the way across Australia. A considerable feat in those days!

What's in a name?

Author Darrell Lewis went in search of the boab tree where the nameplate was found. He travelled into the remote Sturt Creek area, where the gun was said to have been discovered. After examining hundreds of trees, he was unable to find one with an L carved on it. It's possible that the letter wasn't there in the first place, or that the tree has since died. Even after the search area was expanded, no tree matching the description of that particular boab tree was found – which doesn't mean it doesn't exist. It's feasible that it may exist outside of the search area, or that it was missed in the search.

The nameplate itself, however, offered researchers a great deal of information. Scientists from the Western Australian Museum carried out scanning electron microscope tests of the plate to learn more about its history. (A scanning electron microscope creates an image of the sample being viewed by scanning it with a beam of electrons.) The researchers learned that the brass was indeed from the early 1800s: sulphur residues on the plate matched the type of gunpowder used in those days, and various chemical changes showed that the plate had been in an arid location for a long period of time.

Although they learned a lot from the electron microscope tests, Dr Lewis believes the nameplate could offer even more information if further tests were carried out. For example, he suggests that it may contain pollen from plants that are only found in certain parts of Australia. If so, it would settle once and for all the debate over which route the expedition took. Other organic material on the plate could also help to pinpoint the path the party took. The extraction of such material can be performed by a process called micro-excavation. Researchers are hopeful that this and other tests will be carried out in the not-too-distant future, allowing them to slowly piece together the answer to a mystery over 160 years old.

PRIME MINISTER HAROLD HOLT

The 17th Prime Minister of Australia entered the water for a swim at Cheviot Beach one day and was never seen again. The official story is that he was swept away and drowned. As for the unofficial stories . . . Could any of the bizarre rumours be true?

A nation-changing leader

Harold Holt became prime minister and leader of the Liberal Party when Sir Robert Menzies retired in January 1966. Holt's time in office was short, but he is remembered for his nation-changing policies. His prime ministership saw a weakening of Australia's focus on Britain, as Holt strove to forge closer ties with America. Declaring 'All the way with LBJ' (America's President Johnson), Holt increased Australia's commitment to the Vietnam War. This was the year when we converted to a decimal currency, forgoing

English-style pounds, shilling and pence for American-like dollars and cents.

Holt's era also made our nation more inclusive. The White Australia policy, which previously only welcomed migrants from Europe, was altered to allow refugees from war-torn Vietnam to enter. And in 1967, a referendum successfully changed the Australian Constitution to remove references that discriminated against Indigenous Australians.

Despite all that, Holt is best remembered for his mysterious disappearance one summer's afternoon.

On 17 December 1967, the prime minister entered the water at Cheviot Beach near Portsea, Victoria. He was a strong swimmer and knew the beach well. Turbulent conditions made his companions keep to the shallows, but Harold Holt strode confidently out into the deeper waters. Ignoring his friends' warnings about the rough sea, he disappeared from view . . . and was never seen again.

Rumours run riot

The search that took place was among the largest in Australian history, but no trace was found of the prime minister. Two days later, the government declared him dead and a funeral was arranged.

At the time there was no coroner's inquiry into Harold Holt's death. This may well have sparked the beginning of the conspiracy theories – but there's a simple reason why it didn't happen. In the 1960s, the law in Victoria didn't allow the coroner to investigate cases where there was no body. Decades later the law was changed, and when it did an inquiry took place. In 2005 the coroner finally declared that the prime minister had drowned while swimming.

The lack of a coronial inquiry in the 1960s doesn't mean the case wasn't thoroughly investigated by the police. The official view then, like now, was that Holt had drowned. You can view the police reports yourself on the National Archives' website: see 'Want more?' on page 230 for details.

UFOs, spies and mysterious murders

The rumours persisted, regardless of the fact that the police reports were released to the public. Some people thought Harold Holt was abducted by a UFO. (Keep in mind Holt disappeared at a time when the Space Race between the United States and the Soviet Union was in full swing. With all this focus on space, UFOs were constantly in the popular imagination and UFO sightings made the news more than once.) Other people think he faked his own death in order to run off with a supposed girl-friend. Still, others think he had been depressed and didn't want to return home.

One of the most interesting rumours was that Holt was a Chinese spy. This was the basis of the book *The Prime Minister was a Spy* by British author Anthony Grey. The idea was that the prime minister didn't drown. Instead, he was picked up by a submarine and taken to China, where he remained for the rest of his life. The source of this information was a naval officer who wanted to remain anonymous. When Holt's widow heard the rumour, she dismissed it as ridiculous. Her husband couldn't have gone to China, she said. He didn't even like Chinese food!

There's another theory that's possibly even more bizarre. A man called Gary Simmons believes the prime minister was deliberately murdered. Why? Simmons claims that Holt opposed the building of Pine Gap, a secret American military base in the Northern Territory, and that this led to his death. Gary Simmons claims that the version of events given by Harold Holt's friends was wrong. Holt wasn't out swimming that morning. Rather, he was killed the night before he officially disappeared – Simmons himself saw the dead body! Simmons states he was employed to pick up the prime minister's dead body and take it out to a waiting fishing boat. He is very vehement about his beliefs, but hasn't been taken seriously by the authorities.

This might all sound very odd, but there's something equally odd that is undoubtedly true. A swimming pool in Victoria was named after the drowned man – the Harold Holt Swim Centre!

The Bass Strait connection, plus a shipwreck

If you've read the section about the Bass Strait Triangle on page 78, you'll know that many people, boats and aircraft have gone missing there. Could the disappearance of Harold Holt be yet another mystery to add to the long list of Bass Strait disappearances?

Cheviot Beach, where the Prime Minister vanished, is on the Point Nepean Peninsula. This marks the southern point of The Rip – turbulent waters that connect Port Phillip to the Bass Strait. Waters in the area can be dangerous, especially when the tide rises in the strait.

Interestingly, Cheviot Beach gets its name from a shipwreck that occurred back in 1887. The iron steamship *Cheviot* was making its way through Port Phillip Heads when disaster struck. Its propeller hit an underwater rock and snapped off. The ship was pushed onto a reef and broke in two within just 15 minutes. There were 59 passengers and crew, and sadly 35 people didn't survive the accident.

BABY AZARIA CHAMBERLAIN

A baby vanished at Uluru under mysterious circumstances. Her disappearance made headlines and divided a nation. Was she murdered by her mother or taken by a dingo?

A cry in the dark

The events of 17 August 1980 caused heartbreak for a young family and sparked a debate that raged for years. It seemed that everybody had an opinion about what had happened on that fateful night. It took many years for the truth to come out, and there are still people who refuse to believe the official findings and cling to their first impressions. That's probably because the story is so bizarre!

The Chamberlain family – Michael, Lindy, and their three young children – had gone on a camping trip to Uluru (then called Ayers Rock) in the Northern Territory. Arriving on 16 August, they drove to a camp site and pitched a tent next to their car.

The next evening, they were sitting with other holiday-makers and chatting. At about 8 pm, Lindy Chamberlain thought she heard her nine-week-old baby cry out. She went to their tent to investigate and to her horror found the baby missing. Lindy said she saw a dingo coming out of the tent, which hadn't been zipped up properly. There were dingo tracks in and around the tent. Blood was later found on various items inside it, including the carry basket the baby had been sleeping in.

Could a dingo have taken her baby? Was Lindy's incredible story possible? Such a thing had never been heard of before. Both Indigenous and non-Indigenous trackers were quickly sent off to search for Azaria, but sadly she was never found. Suspicion about her tragic death didn't immediately fall on the mother – but it didn't take long for the rumours to start.

The evidence

One week later, most of baby Azaria's clothes were found in the wilderness. The strange thing was that her jumpsuit, booties, nappy and singlet seemed to have been left in a neat pile. Could a dingo have removed the infant's clothing and arranged them in this way? Or did this evidence suggest a human hand? Furthermore, even though the jumpsuit was bloodstained and torn, there was no dingo saliva on it and it appeared to show the shape of a handprint. Importantly, the matinee jacket (a knitted cardigan) that Lindy Chamberlain said the baby was wearing wasn't with the rest of the clothing. (We'll come back to why this was significant later.)

In February the following year, the coroner found that Azaria was taken by a dingo, and that her clothing had been interfered with by an unknown person. But the police were not

The Chamberlains with a photograph of baby Azaria,
who they claimed was killed by a dingo.

satisfied with this. More evidence was sought and examined, and in November a second coroner's inquest committed Lindy Chamberlain to trial for murder. Her husband was charged as an accessory after the fact – meaning it was thought he had helped his wife cover up evidence of her crime.

So why did the police claim that Lindy Chamberlain was guilty? It came down to forensic evidence, which supposedly revealed blood spatters inside the family car. Could this be proof of foul play? It was also thought that Azaria's jumpsuit had been cut by scissors, not dingo claws. Could Lindy have been trying to hide what she did by making those 'dingo' claw marks herself? But there was more to it than that. Lindy Chamberlain didn't come across well in the media. She didn't seem to be displaying the emotions expected of a grieving mother. Instead, she was seen as cold, detached and unfeeling. This – as well as the unlikeliness of her story – had the effect of swaying public opinion against her.

It put pressure on the police to convict the 'real' killer, who many believed to be Azaria's mother.

Of course, not everybody shows their feelings in the same way, so Lindy Chamberlain's reaction can hardly be called evidence of guilt. It's hard to know how you're going to react to tragedy until you're faced with it yourself – a reminder to always look beyond appearances.

Lindy Chamberlain's trial began in September 1982. Heavily pregnant, she was found guilty of the murder of Azaria and was sentenced to life imprisonment. Her new baby was taken away from her and given to a foster family. Lindy's husband, Michael, was found guilty as an accessory after the fact. He received an 18-month suspended sentence. (A suspended sentence is not served unless a further offence is committed.)

Throughout all this, the Chamberlains maintained that they weren't guilty, that they hadn't done it. Years of appeals and petitions followed, but it took an additional piece of evidence to finally turn things around.

A surprising discovery

The defence maintained that the evidence relied upon in court was flawed. The blood test results were challenged, the defence claiming that no blood had been found in the family car after all. Instead, they insisted the substance tested was a mixture of sound deadener, milkshake and copper dust. It also came out that Azaria's clothing had actually been found scrunched, not neatly folded, and was handled before being photographed. But what really caused shockwaves was the finding of Azaria's matinee jacket in February 1986.

The matinee jacket was found quite by accident. A rock climber had fallen, and the jacket was discovered while rescuers were searching for him. The finding was important, because it explained why dingo saliva had not been found on the jumpsuit – the saliva would have been on the jacket which Azaria was wearing over her jumpsuit. Although saliva was not found on the jacket, this might be because it was discovered too late and any evidence had been washed away by rain. Even so, it was this discovery that started a chain of events that finally led to Lindy Chamberlain's release from gaol the following year. All up, she spent three years in gaol.

A movie starring Meryl Streep as Lindy Chamberlain was made soon after, bringing the world's attention to this tragic Australian story. The film was called *Evil Angels* (released under

the title *A Cry in the Dark* in the United States). Dingo jokes proliferated, both in Australia and overseas. Several high-profile American comedies, including *Seinfeld* and *The Simpsons*, made jokes about dingoes eating babies – perhaps not realising the film was based on a true story!

Even though Lindy Chamberlain had been released from gaol, it took a Royal Commission and further inquests to settle the matter once and for all. Finally, in 2012, the coroner found that baby Azaria wasn't murdered. According to the official verdict, she had indeed been taken by a dingo.

Bizarre rumours

Many strange rumours circulated during the investigations and trials, adding fuel to the bad public opinion of the mother. Lindy Chamberlain-Creighton, as she is now called, described them in her book *Through My Eyes: An Autobiography* and on her website. The rumours included:

- Azaria means 'sacrifice in the wilderness'. Rather, Lindy found it in a baby names book where it was said to mean 'blessed of God'.
- Azaria was always dressed in black. While it's true Lindy and Michael had at times dressed their baby in black, unusual personal taste is hardly proof of murder!
- The Chamberlains had underlined a passage in their Bible about a woman who drove a tent peg through a man's head, thereby killing him. They hadn't.

THE SS WARATAH

The steamship SS *Waratah* was built to transport passengers and cargo between England and Australia. In July 1909, on what was only the ship's second journey, it vanished without trace. Is it possible that its name was cursed, and that it really was followed by a ghost ship?

The *Titanic* of the south

The SS *Waratah* was a luxury liner that has been compared to the *Titanic*. Both of these grand ships were hailed as being unsink-able – and both shared the same tragic fate. But while the remains of the *Titanic* have been found and studied, the resting place of the *Waratah* is still a mystery.

The *Waratah* left Australia on her second voyage. She was to return to faraway England via South Africa. It was between the South African ports of Durban and Cape Town that the ship went missing, failing to dock as expected. The Royal Navy sent cruisers to search for her, as did the ship's owners, the Blue Anchor line . . . But to no avail.

Missing ships aren't that uncommon. What makes this disappearance so interesting are the bizarre circumstances surrounding it.

Dreams, cursed names and ghost ships

On reaching Durban, one passenger disembarked from the *Waratah* and refused to get back on. An experienced ocean traveller, Claude Sawyer felt that the ship was top-heavy, which made him anxious. What really worried him, however, was a strange dream he'd had. Sawyer told a newspaper he'd dreamed he was standing on the ship's deck, looking out to sea, when a knight on a horse rose out of the waves. A bloodstained sheet fluttered behind the knight, who was swinging a sword and screaming 'Waratah!'. Sawyer told other passengers about his dream but they refused to take it seriously.

Might the passengers have paid more attention to Sawyer's fears if they'd known what had happened to other ships called *Waratah*? The *Weird Australia* website lists the sad history of other ships named for the floral emblem of New South Wales. Several ships, all called *Waratah*, were lost during the second half of the 19th century, taking many lives. Could the name of this strikingly beautiful flower be cursed? Most likely it was a coincidence – ships with other names sank too. Still, there are plenty of other names that could have been chosen instead!

There's another odd thing worth mentioning. The day after it left Durban, the SS *Waratah* was seen by the freighter *Clan McIntyre*. They exchanged signals and continued on their way. So far, so good. But then the captain of the freighter saw something that made his blood run cold . . .

Behind the *Waratah,* following as if in pursuit, was another ship. But it was no ordinary ship! An old-fashioned sailing vessel, its outdated rigging matched that of the infamous *Flying Dutchman* – a ghost ship that foretells doom. The experienced and respected captain was astounded. He didn't consider himself a superstitious man, but he was familiar with the legend. As he watched the ghostly ship vanish before his eyes, he couldn't shake the feeling that disaster would soon befall the liner. But more about the creepy legend of the *Flying Dutchman* later . . .

Catching sight of the *Flying Dutchman* is said to be a portent of doom.

Freak wave or freak out?

So what happened to the ship? There is no shortage of theories. In his book *The Lost Ship SS Waratah: The Search for The Titanic of the South*, PJ Smith notes that the most commonly held view was that a freak wave overwhelmed the *Waratah*. Giant waves are relatively common in that part of the ocean. Combined with a severe storm, a freak wave might have been enough to make the ship capsize or roll over completely. If debris became trapped under the ship, it would sink with it, explaining why no wreckage was ever found.

Another view is that a freak wave caused the ship to capsize, killing everyone on board, and then drift southwards towards Antarctica – again explaining the lack of wreckage. Other theories include the ship disappearing into a whirlpool, an explosion in one of the ship's coal bunkers, and a methane upwelling (gas rising up from the sea bed that makes the water too dense for a ship to float).

Of course there are paranormal explanations too, suggesting that ghosts or evil spirits lured the ship's passengers and crew to their deaths. It may be fanciful, but it's not too surprising people think this way, given Claude Sawyer's freaky dream and the freighter captain's sighting of the famous ghost ship the *Flying Dutchman*.

Interest in the fate of the *Waratah* continues to this day. Pieces of cork and timber that might have belonged to the liner were washed up in South Africa in the 1930s, but it couldn't be established with any certainty that they were in fact from that ship. In 1999, newspapers reported that a search team had located a wreck whose outline matched that of the *Waratah*. Again, this was off the coast of South Africa. A closer inspection two years later, however, concluded that the wreckage actually belonged to another ship that had been sunk during World War II. It may well be that a future search crew will one day unearth the remains, but for now, we can't know for sure what happened to the ship!

The Flying Dutchman

The spooky story of the *Flying Dutchman* originates from 17th-century nautical folklore. Legend has it that a crazed Dutch captain was trying to sail around South Africa's Cape of Good Hope, a difficult thing at the best of times. A wild gale was blowing and the winds were very rough. The crew begged the captain to turn back but he refused. Mad or drunk (or both!), he sang crude songs and held his course.

His frightened crew rebelled. A mutiny sprang up, but the captain brutally suppressed it, killing the leader and throwing him overboard. A shadowy figure then appeared on deck, sternly reproaching the captain for being a foolish man. The captain had no qualms about shooting at this figure too, but his gun misfired. Unfazed, the shadowy figure kept on talking. He cursed the captain and the crew, saying they would never make port and were doomed to sail forever, even after their deaths. A dead crew on an endless journey on a ghost ship. Oh yes, and if anyone ever saw the ship, death and disaster would surely follow!

THE *High Aim 6*

You may have heard of the mysterious *Mary Celeste*, a sailing ship found drifting in the Atlantic with nobody on board. You might not have heard of the *High Aim 6*, a fishing boat that suffered a similar fate in Australian waters. What could have made the entire crew vanish without trace?

An abandoned boat

On 4 January 2003, a team of Australian customs agents were on a routine mission, checking the seas for people smugglers and illegal fishing boats. They spotted the Taiwanese-owned boat the *High Aim 6* in the Indian Ocean. The customs agents couldn't see anybody on board, but they didn't think that was too strange. The crew might have been below deck. Even so, they filed a report. The ship was in the Australian fishing zone, where foreign fishing is restricted. A close eye would have to be kept on the boat. Little did they know that within days it would be found to be crewless, reeking of death and decay.

The *High Aim 6* left Taiwan on 31 October (Halloween!) 2002. It had a Taiwanese captain and chief engineer and an Indonesian crew. The last time the boat made radio contact was on 13 December, while passing the Marshall Islands in the Pacific Ocean. Something happened between that date and early January. Something that nobody can explain . . .

On 9 January 2003, the Australian naval vessel the HMAS *Stuart* encountered the ship off the coast of Broome, Western Australia. Puzzled by the boat's aimless drifting, they boarded it to investigate. What they found was described by John Pinkney in his book *The Mary Celeste Syndrome: Ships From Which all Human Life has Vanished*.

The group were greeted by an overpowering stench of decay. Fearing the worst, they tracked the eye-watering smell to the boat's hold. Fortunately they didn't find a dead crew. Rather, they found several tonnes of rotting fish. The fishing boat's freezer had clearly stopped working when the engines shut down, but nobody knew why the engines had stopped – and this was only the start of the puzzle.

On the dash of the wheelhouse (an enclosed area where a person stands to steer the boat) they found a pair of glasses, a jar of coffee and an opened packet of cigarettes. Toothbrushes were hung neatly on their racks. Clothes were folded and stored in lockers, along with the crew's all-important identification documents. Wallets containing cash and other personal effects were left behind. There was ample food, water and fuel. All that was missing was the people. Where could they have gone?

It looked as though the captain had only stepped away
from his post for a short time.

An intensive search over a 25,000-kilometre stretch was carried out, but there was no trace of the captain or crew.

No sign of struggle

So what happened to the crew? The *High Aim 6* was towed to a quarantine bay off Broome, where the Australian Federal Police conducted an investigation. Various theories were considered, each quickly rejected.

The most obvious theory was that the crew had run out of food, water or fuel, and had been forced to abandon ship. But there was plenty to eat and drink and the fuel tanks were half-full. Interestingly, no life raft was found on board. Did that mean the crew had escaped on it? It's not certain. It's not uncommon for boats such as this to not have life rafts, regardless of legal requirements. But if the crew had escaped on a raft, where were they, and why weren't they found during the thorough search?

Could pirates have taken hold of the ship, killing the crew and throwing them overboard? That seemed unlikely. There was no sign of a struggle, and pirates would most likely have taken off with the ship – not to mention the money, equipment and valuable identification documents.

No plausible solution was reached to explain what had happened to the crew of the ghost ship *High Aim 6*.

Finally, there was no sign of the sort of damage that might have been caused by a rogue wave.

Suspicions were raised that the boat had been carrying immigrants hoping to claim asylum in Australia. The hold full of fish, however, suggested otherwise. The *High Aim 6* appeared to be a legitimate fishing vessel rather than a people-smuggling boat.

No plausible explanation

After eight months of investigation, the Australian Federal Police declared they could find no plausible explanation for why the ship had been abandoned. The investigators handed over control of the boat to the Australian Fisheries Management Authority. The Taiwanese owners didn't want it back, claiming it would be too expensive to repair. It's also possible they suspected they wouldn't be able to find a crew willing to board the death ship! Nobody wanted it hanging around, and the fishing boat's final fate was to be dismantled and discarded.

An interesting update to the mystery appeared in the Taiwanese newspaper *The Taipei Times* on 22 January 2003. According to the family of the chief engineer, Lin Chung-li, his mobile phone had been used repeatedly between 1 and 10 January – *after* the boat had been found abandoned. The calls were made in Bali, Indonesia, racking up a huge bill. Also, the Indonesian police arrested a suspect who admitted he was one of the crew members. It wasn't clear whether this was the person who'd allegedly been using the engineer's mobile. The suspect said both the captain and chief engineer had been killed and that the rest of the crew had fled and headed back to Indonesia. The reports do not explain how the captain and engineer were killed, neither do they give a motive for the mutiny, if that's what it was. There is no explanation of how the crew got to Indonesia, why they left the ship in the state that it was found, nor why they left their wallets and papers behind. Unfortunately, not much light was shed on the mystery by this confession.

The Mary Celeste *and more*

The *High Aim 6* has been compared to the *Mary Celeste*, the most famous abandoned ship. This American brigantine left New York on 7 November 1872, heading for Genoa in Italy. On 4 December it was spotted with its sails set, moving erratically through the Atlantic Ocean near the Azores Islands. There was nobody at the wheel, and investigators found meals half-eaten and personal belongings left undisturbed. It looked as if everyone had simply evaporated!

Countless documentaries have been made about the mystery, with the most remarkable solutions suggested. Alien abductions, sea monsters, portals into different dimensions ... It seems the wilder the ideas, the more people like them!

More rational theories have also emerged. These include concerns that the crew had eaten spoiled food, sending them mad. An examination of the food knocked that idea on the head, however. A similar belief was that fumes escaping from the cargo (alcohol stored in barrels) drove them all crazy, although this has never been proved. A more plausible idea was that escaping alcohol fumes caused an explosion. Even though no soot or other signs of scorching were found, researchers have demon-strated that a pressure-wave explosion does not necessarily leave signs of burning behind it. But would it be enough to make everyone abandon ship – with or without lifeboats – and be unable to get back on again afterwards?

Whatever the answer, it seems that the *Mary Celeste* and the *High Aim 6* are not alone. In his book, Pinkney identifies several other ships that have shared the same fate. He calls it the Mary Celeste Syndrome. In each case:

- The ship was found drifting through the ocean with nobody on board.
- The ship's systems were intact and there was no sign of significant damage.
- Food and water supplies were adequate.
- Valuables were undisturbed.
- There were no signs of violence, either from intruders or from bad weather.

Let's just hope it doesn't happen again!

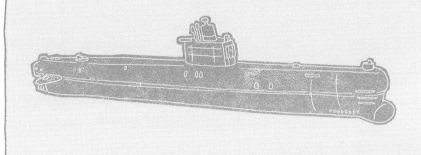

MALAYSIA AIRLINES FLIGHT 370

Nobody expected that a modern commercial aeroplane could vanish without trace. But in 2014, that's exactly what happened to MH370. What could have caused this shocking tragedy?

A disappearance that stunned the world

At 41 minutes past midnight on 8 March 2014, Malaysia Airlines Flight 370 (MH370) departed Kuala Lumpur airport. It was due to arrive in Beijing at 6.30 that morning. The aeroplane never arrived and – at the time of writing – it has still not been found. How can such a thing occur in modern times? Flight technology and communication systems have become so sophisticated, it's hard to understand how a jet airliner carrying 227 passengers and 12 crew can simply disappear. So what happened?

About one hour into the flight, the plane sent its last ACARS (Aircraft Communications Addressing and Reporting System) transmission. This is a service that allows the plane's computers to communicate with computers on the ground. Less than 15 minutes later, the pilot or copilot uttered the last words spoken to Malaysian air traffic control: 'Good night Malaysian three seven zero'. Soon afterwards the plane's transponder (which communicates with ground radar) stopped working. The plane was expected to check in with Vietnamese air traffic control at 1.20 am but failed to do so.

For an unknown reason, it changed direction. Diverting from its planned route, the plane turned and headed west out over the Indian Ocean. We know this because the plane was initially tracked by Malaysian and Thai military radar. After that, MH370 continued to 'ping' or signal its location to satellites. It did this automatically every hour for seven hours. There was one last partial communication with the satellite, meaning that the aircraft sent a request to a ground station to log on. Investigators explained that this is the sort of thing that can happen after there's been an interruption to the aircraft's electrical supply. Then . . . absolutely nothing.

Complications and confusion

Confusion about what had happened to the plane partly arose because it took such a long time for any information to be revealed. Even the fact that the plane was missing was not publicly announced for several hours. It took days for crucial information to emerge, such as the sighting on military radar, which led to the wrong areas being searched, wasting valuable time. Right or wrong, there was a feeling that the Malaysian authorities were being secretive and not sharing what they knew.

Contradictory information was given out to the families of the missing passengers, adding to their already extreme distress. Indeed, the Malaysian government faced a lot of criticism for its handling of the matter. For example, it was wrongly stated that the last words by the pilots to air traffic control were, 'All right, good night'. Such a response would have been unusual and unprofessional. Why would an experienced pilot talk so informally, rather than using the correct words? It raised suspicions that either the pilot or the copilot was deliberately ignoring protocol and might have been planning to crash the plane on purpose – maybe as an act of terrorism or suicide. However, after learning more about the background and experience of the pilots, this was later discounted as unlikely, and of course the words were never spoken in the first place!

After the plane's disappearance, the backgrounds of everyone on the flight were thoroughly investigated, including the flight crew. It was discovered that two of the passengers were Iranians using false passports. Again, this raised the question of a terrorist attack. Were these passengers on a terror watch list, and so wanted to use fake passports in an attempt to avoid detection? In the end, however, the information gathered led investigators to the conclusion that the Iranian passengers were most likely attempting to migrate illegally.

A double mystery

There are two key unanswered questions about the missing flight. First, what caused the plane to disappear? And second, where did it go?

In her book *The Mystery of Malaysia Airlines Flight 370*, Sylvia Wrigley considered the possibilities. She explained the various ways in which planes can be damaged and how the pilots would be likely to react. If the pilots were aware of the danger and capable of responding to it, Wrigley suggests that the most probable course would be for them to try to land. The thing that's so odd about flight MH370 is that the plane continued to fly for seven hours after it went off course. If there had been a catastrophic failure, for instance due to a large explosion caused either deliberately or by accident, why didn't the plane crash quickly? Similarly, if the pilot or someone else used the plane to commit suicide, why didn't it happen more quickly? It's unlikely they would have continued to fly for seven hours, in which time they could have been stopped by others.

Sylvia Wrigley believes it plausible that the plane was at first deliberately diverted, perhaps due to a hijacking, but then something else went wrong, something that caused people to lose consciousness. There could have been a small explosion or a gunshot, which led to a slow loss of air pressure. Oxygen levels would have dropped, making people on board lose consciousness. This could be why the plane continued to fly on autopilot until it ran out of fuel.

Wrigley emphasised, however, that nothing can be certain until the wreckage is found. The wreckage could then be studied and the damage would provide essential clues. All commercial planes carry black boxes (which are actually bright orange so they're more easily spotted) that record and store information. There are two separate recorders. One is a cockpit voice recorder, which records conversations and other sounds. The second is a flight data recorder that stores information about the plane's systems. Black boxes are activated if a plane crashes or becomes submerged in water. They give out signals to help them be found, but the signals only last about 30 days. Finding them quickly is always a priority.

Which leads to the second question: where did the plane go? An analysis of the satellite pings provided researchers with a possible flight path. The most likely scenario was that MH370 flew south over the Indian Ocean, crashing off the West Australian coast. This sparked a massive search effort, in which the Australian Maritime Safety Authority played a leading role.

Excitement grew in early April when it was believed that the black box's signals had been detected. Sadly, a thorough search of the ocean floor in that area failed to find it before the signals ended just days later. Keep in mind that the search area was huge – it was expanded to 12 square kilometres – and in rough waters far from the coast, so it would have been a very difficult operation.

On 29 July 2015 a piece of debris was found washed up on Reunion Island in the Indian Ocean. It was identified as being a flaperon (one of the wing control surfaces on an aircraft). The serial number on the flaperon confirmed that it had belonged to MH370. Although far from the search area in Western Australia, the action of ocean currents means it is likely that searchers were on the right track to discover the rest of the wreckage, hopefully including the black box. In March 2016, more pieces were found that might also have come from the plane. It looks like the haystack has been found. Now for the needle!

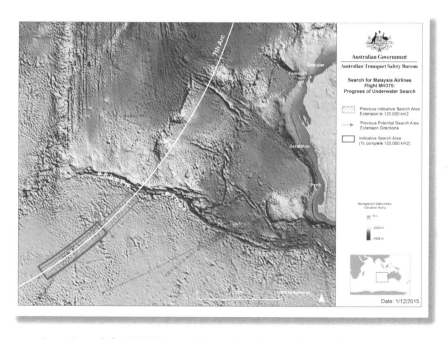

Location of the MH370 search area in the southern Indian Ocean.

In May 2016, Australian authorities announced that the search might soon be called off if more evidence is not found.

As for how and why the accident happened . . . Until the black boxes are found, the rest remains speculation – and even then, we might not find out for sure what exactly took place. For up-to-date information, visit the website of the Joint Agency Coordination Centre. Details are available at 'Want more?' on page 230.

Conspiracies galore

As with any mystery, conspiracy theories concerning the fate of MH370 thrived. Sylvia Wrigley analysed them one by one in her book. The theories ranged from the reasonably plausible to the wildly imaginative. The wildest was the idea that the plane was abducted by aliens!

Other theories included the possibility that the plane was shot down by the military, and this has indeed happened in other cases. Piracy, kidnapping and hijacking theories have also spread around the globe. Most kidnappers or hijackers, however, draw attention to what they have done, hoping to have their demands met. Even terrorists tend to admit responsibility for their actions, as their intention is to instil fear in the public.

Until solid evidence is found, it seems that the conspiracy theories surrounding this modern-day mystery will continue to spread.

WANT MORE?

For more information about these and other bizarre disappearances, have a look at:

- Australian Transport Safety Bureau's website, regarding the search for MH370, at https://www.atsb.gov.au/mh370.aspx

- Chamberlain-Creighton L, *Through My Eyes: The Autobiography of Lindy Chamberlain-Creighton*, Heinemann, 1990

- Frame T, *The Life and Death of Harold Holt*, Allen & Unwin, 2005

- Lewis D, *Where is Dr Leichhardt? The Greatest Mystery in Australian History*, Monash University Press, 2013

- National Archives of Australia website, showing a digital copy of *Search for Mr Holt – arrangements including report by Victorian and Commonwealth police*, http://www.naa.gov.au/collection/fact-sheets/fs144.aspx

- Pinkney J, *The Mary Celeste Syndrome: Ships From Which all Human Life has Vanished,* Inkypen Editions, 2011

- Smith PJ, *The Lost Ship SS Waratah: Searching for the Titanic of the South,* History Press, 2009

- Wrigley S, *The Mystery of Malaysia Airlines Flight 370,* E-quality Press, 2014

STRANGE HAPPENINGS

Some Australian myths and mysteries are so strange, it's hard to know how to categorise them. That's certainly the case with the weird occurrences described in this final chapter. They stand alone as some of the most puzzling things ever to have happened in this country. Murdered horses, human torches, four-kilometre-long drawings, hieroglyphic carvings and ancient African coins . . . All so different, yet all so mysterious!

It's worth saying again that when you consider any puzzling claim, it's important to keep an open mind. Refusing to consider something just because it's unusual means you might be missing out on some very useful information. It's equally important to judge things intelligently, however, or else you run the risk of being seriously mistaken and perhaps falling for a scam. Part of this process is understanding the difference between a science and a pseudoscience.

'Pseudo' is from the Greek word for 'fake'. A pseudoscience might look like a real science, but it doesn't use true scientific methods. True scientists challenge their own claims and try to find evidence that might prove that the claims are wrong. If something cannot be disproven, then perhaps it has validity.

On the other hand, pseudoscientists seek results that confirm rather than challenge their claims. The results of pseudoscientists also aren't verifiable. That is, the results aren't able to be tested and reproduced by others. The claims rely heavily on rumours, anecdotes and unverified witness testimony. A good example is a fat-burning pill that lists newly discovered 'miracle' ingredients. If you research the pill closely, you'll see that there are no scientifically controlled experiments that suggest it actually works, and the only evidence offered is by people who supposedly lost weight by taking the product – which can't be relied on! How do we know that something else didn't cause their weight loss, such as dieting while taking the pills? As scientists say, correlation does not imply causation! (Just because x happened at the same time as y, it doesn't mean x caused y.)

Beware of those who appear to be absolutely certain of their claims without giving evidence to back up their views. They seem so confident that it's easy to be swayed by their convictions, which are often highly emotional. Always try to take the emotion out of their claims and look at things objectively. And remember, if you see LOTS OF CAPITAL LETTERS and lots of exclamation marks in an ad or opinion piece, think again!!!!!!!!!

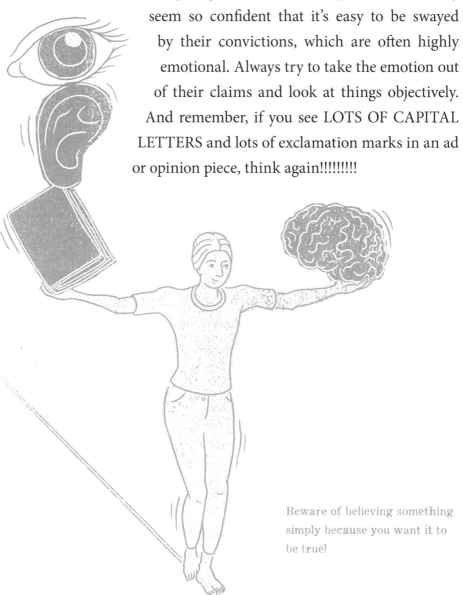

Beware of believing something simply because you want it to be true!

THE HUMAN TORCH

Spontaneous human combustion has been igniting interest for centuries. Is it possible for the human body to suddenly burst into flames for no apparent reason?

Reduced to ashes

In August 1998, Sydney woman Agnes Phillips suddenly caught fire. There was no obvious cause for the blazing flames that led to her death. This disturbing phenomenon, known as spontaneous human combustion (SHC), has puzzled scientists for decades. Can people catch fire even if nothing external set them alight? If so, how? Can people burn from the inside out?

Although SHC is rare, the recorded cases have several features in common. The victim was often (but not always) elderly or frail. Usually, too, the victim was on their own. This is significant for two reasons. One, there was no one to help them put the flames out, and two, there was no one to witness how the fire started nor how long it continued.

But there's more mystery to these grisly stories than might first meet the eye. Here's a warning: only read on if you have a strong stomach! In cases of SHC where help arrived too late, the victims were burned down to mere ash. Even their skeletons were reduced to powder. 'So what?', you might say. 'That's what happens when something burns!' But it's odd when you think about it. Bodies are cremated at temperatures between 700 and 1000 degrees Celsius and the process typically takes one-and-a-half to two-and-a-half hours. Even at these extreme temperatures, bones can remain fairly intact and have to be ground up. Which begs the question: how hot or prolonged does the fire have to be to reduce bones to dust? Does the destruction happen quickly or over many hours? Even more astonishingly, in some cases of SHC, various body parts remained untouched by the fire. Usually this has been the victim's lower legs and feet. Even their trousers, socks and shoes have escaped the flames. How could these be left intact when everything else was ash?

To add to the mystery, the rooms the victims were in weren't destroyed by the fire. You might expect the whole house to burn down – but no. Generally there would just be some scorching beneath the body. Soot may have covered the walls or ceiling, but most objects in the room remained unburned. Plastics, however, were often found melted, showing that the room reached extremely high temperatures.

In the case of Sydney woman Agnes Phillips, things didn't get this far. Her story is still horrific, however. The key difference here is that Mrs Phillips, who suffered from dementia and lived in a nursing home, was only left alone for a short time. Her daughter Jackie had picked her up to take her for a day out. Jackie left her mother asleep in the car while quickly popping into the shops. Not long afterwards, Jackie noticed smoke billowing from the car.

In some cases of spontaneous human combustion, the body is mysteriously reduced to ashes . . . except for the feet!

A passer-by managed to drag Agnes Phillips out of the car and extinguish the flames. Sadly, Mrs Phillips suffered severe burns and died a week later in hospital.

The cause of the fire was a mystery. The fire inspector in this case was quoted in the newspapers as saying he couldn't determine where or how the fire started. The engine wasn't running, so there would have been no heat, petrol fumes or errant sparks coming from the engine. There appeared to be no faulty wiring, and neither mother nor daughter were smokers. There was no trace of flammable liquids on Mrs Phillips' body and it was a cool winter's day. The inspector suggested it had been caused by the wick effect – but more on that later!

Possible causes – or possibly not?

Cases of SHC have been reported all over the world, sparking ongoing debates. Scientists believe something must be causing the initial flames, and that bodies don't burn without reason. Others, such as Larry Arnold, the author of *Ablaze! The Mysterious Fires of Spontaneous Human Combustion*, is dismayed by the scientific world's scepticism. He claims to be an expert on the subject, and believes it *is* possible for people to just burst into flames.

Arnold proposes the existence of subatomic particles called pyrotrons. Supposedly these tiny particles zip around in the spaces between the quarks (particles of matter smaller than atoms) that are everywhere, including in our bodies. Very rarely, a rogue pyrotron hits a quark. This can set off a chain reaction that may result in SHC. Larry Arnold calls this the Internal Hiroshima Effect. It sounds impressive – and at first glance appears to be based on quantum physics – but scientists do not recognise the existence of pyrotrons and do not believe that people can catch fire from within.

Mind you, Larry Arnold has other theories, too, about what may cause SHC. One involves a type of energy that is said to flow up and down people's spinal columns. Known as kundalini energy, it is based on spiritual yoga philosophies. Arnold believes that if this energy becomes unbalanced, for instance by emotional distress, it can produce powerful energy spikes. A ball of energy can form in the abdomen, reducing the body to ash but leaving the legs and arms unharmed.

His third theory involves mystical lines of earth energy that supposedly flow around the planet. Arnold calls this his 'cartography of combustion' theory. It is based on his observations that, if plotted on a map, many instances of mysterious fires in the United Kingdom can be connected by straight lines. He says the idea is similar to that of ley lines, which are geographical alignments said to form links between ancient monuments. Arnold believes these lines follow flows of energy that move through the earth. He says that under the right conditions, these energy flows can cause spontaneous combustion in property and people.

The BBC documentary series QED (*quod erat demonstrandum* – Latin for 'that which was to be proved') took a more scientific approach to the puzzle. In the SHC episode, it brought together fire experts from around the world, who considered various scientific theories. These included being struck by ball lightning (a rare but real phenomenon), the action of bacteria and enzymes, and a build-up of methane gas inside the gut. None of these theories, however, could offer a complete explanation for what has been observed in SHC cases. Instead, the show went on to explain that SHC cases can most likely be explained by the wick effect.

The wick effect

In order to burn, a fire needs three things:

1. Oxygen. No mystery there, it's in the air.

2. Ignition. This could be a match, a cigarette, an ember from a fire, or a spark from a stove or heater. Scientists believe that in all cases of supposed SHC, there must have been an external ignition source, even if it wasn't immediately obvious.

3. Fuel. This is where things get gross. Skip this bit if you just had lunch!

The *QED* documentary compared the human body to an inside-out candle. Clothes can act like a wick. The 'wax' (that is, the fuel) is the body's own fat. When the fat starts to melt, it seeps into the clothing and feeds the fire. If no one is able to put out the flames, the body can continue to burn steadily for many hours. Long enough to crumble bone.

But can this theory explain the other bizarre features of SHC cases, such as how bones were reduced to ash yet legs and feet were left undamaged? An experiment was performed by Dr John de Haan of the California Criminalistics Institute to see if he could replicate what might happen in an apparently spontaneous combustion. He wrapped a dead pig in a blanket (to simulate a person wearing clothes) and placed it in an enclosed space that replicated an average living room in size, containing common household items. The blanket was set alight. After five hours of continuous burning, the pig's skeleton began to crumble. The flames produced were small and didn't spread to other objects, but the high heat levels in the room melted plastic objects, just as in cases of supposed SHC. The wick effect even explains how lower legs and feet can remain unburned – they simply don't contain enough fat to continue to fuel the fire. So does this mean that there is no such thing as spontaneous human combustion?

What the Dickens!

Charles Dickens was an English novelist who lived during the 19th century. The author of classics such as *Oliver Twist*, *A Christmas Carol*, and *A Tale of Two Cities*, he's considered one of the greatest writers of the Victorian era.

During that time, many people believed that drinking too much alcohol could cause a person to spontaneously combust. In his story *Bleak House*, published in the 1850s, Dickens used SHC to describe the death of a heavy drinker. Although we now know that being an alcoholic does not make a person suddenly burst into flames, there's actually a good reason why people believed such things.

A heavy drinker might spill alcohol on themselves. Alcohol is of course highly flammable, which means that the clothes would be more easily set alight. If we take the wick effect as a plausible explanation, every case of SHC is not actually spontaneous at all. There needs to be a source of ignition, and the fire takes a long time to cause the damage seen. Lots of people at this time smoked, and with alcohol-soaked clothes, it wouldn't have taken much to start the fire. But there's more.

Most cases of complete SHC happen when the victim is on their own and unable to put out the flames. This might be because they are old and frail. They might have fallen over and knocked themselves unconscious, or maybe the shock of catching alight brought on a heart attack. In the case of heavy drinkers, they might be simply too drunk to save themselves.

So Dickens was partly right, even if for the wrong reasons!

THE DEATH OF PHAR LAP

An Australian icon, this famous racehorse met with a mysterious death in America. Was the big winner really murdered by the mafia?

A remarkable champion

Named after the Thai word for lightning, Phar Lap was a champion racehorse during the dark days of the Great Depression. He was foaled in New Zealand in October 1926, but trained and raced in Australia. His trainer and strapper (a person who looks after racehorses) was Aaron Treve ('Tommy') Woodcock. Man and horse quickly developed a strong bond, and Woodcock was even said to sleep outside Phar Lap's stable before a big race.

Phar Lap's first race wasn't exactly a success. In fact, he finished last. His next three races were better but not brilliant. He won his first race in the Maiden Juvenile Handicap on

27 April 1929, but this wasn't considered remarkable: none of the other horses had won a race either. Then, in late September of that year, he started beating tougher competition. It took a while for Phar Lap to reach his stride – but once he did, there was no stopping him. As a three-year-old, Phar Lap quickly entered a winning streak.

The horse was so successful, he even made enemies! Book-keepers were losing a fortune in payouts. Could this be why someone went so far as to attempt to murder, or at least maim, Phar Lap? On 1 November 1930, Tommy Woodcock was leading the horse back to the stables. What happened on that spring morning sounds like something out of a gangster movie but it really happened: a drive-by shooting! Gunshots rang out from a car, directed at the horse. Fortunately the would-be assailant missed, and Phar Lap went on to win the Melbourne Stakes later that day. A few days later, he won the Melbourne Cup, Australia's most celebrated horseracing event.

Phar Lap was such a good runner that in 1932 he was shipped to Mexico and entered in the prestigious Agua Caliente race. He won in record time, giving Australia its first taste of international horseracing success. The horse was then taken to a private ranch in California for a rest while his owners considered opportunities for his future. Little did anyone know, he wouldn't have one.

Death of a racing legend

On the morning of 5 April 1932, Tommy Woodcock awoke to find Phar Lap in distress. Phar Lap had a high temperature and Woodcock did all he could to help. The Australian vet who

Phar Lap and his trainer shared a special bond. Around two weeks after this was taken in Mexico, the horse died with his head in Tommy Woodcock's arms.

had travelled with them treated the animal, but sadly Phar Lap became much worse. Later that day, the great horse died in agony.

How could a horse in such good condition suddenly fall ill and die? Autopsies were performed on the body, but couldn't pinpoint the cause of death.

Suspicions immediately arose. Rumours spread that the mafia had poisoned Phar Lap. This isn't as far-fetched as it sounds. In those days, the American mafia was heavily involved in horseracing. They backed certain horses that they expected to win, taking steps to knobble the opposition. They wouldn't have taken kindly to the horse from Down Under running off with the prize money.

Another theory was that the horse had been fed damp oats, bringing on a fatal bout of colic. This was suggested following an autopsy that showed the horse's bowel and stomach were inflamed. Yet another view was that Phar Lap had been accidentally poisoned with arsenic. Nearby trees had been sprayed with an insecticide containing lead arsenate and it may have contaminated the grass that Phar Lap had eaten. The thing was, none of the other horses at the ranch had sickened and died, so this theory was also soon dismissed.

Phar Lap's body was brought back to his grieving nation. His heart, which was unusually large for a horse of his size, went to the Australian Institute of Anatomy in Canberra. His skeleton went to New Zealand's national museum, Te Papa. His hide was mounted on a hollow shell, making the horse appear lifelike. It was initially displayed in the National Museum of Victoria, but can now be seen at the nearby Melbourne Museum.

But the hide has an importance far beyond being a historical attraction. It may well have solved the mystery of how the great horse died . . .

Twenty-first century tests

People weren't prepared to let the mystery of Phar Lap's death rest in peace. In the year 2000, it was speculated that the horse might have died of bacterial poisoning – a type that was still unknown in the 1930s.

Then, in 2006, new research found that Phar Lap had indeed ingested arsenic before he died. This was explored in the ABC's science show *Catalyst*. Researchers Dr Ivan Kempson from the University of South Australia and Dermot Henry, manager of the natural science collections at Museum Victoria, explained that they discovered this by taking samples from Phar Lap's mane. Various substances that are in the blood of living creatures can become incorporated into the hair. These include pollutants, drugs and toxins. Only a few hairs were needed for the analysis, which was done using highly advanced equipment in the United States.

Amazingly, arsenic was found in the hairs, but this may have come from the chemicals used to preserve the hide. To be sure, they tested the hairs of another museum exhibit, a mandrill, and found that its hairs also contained this type of arsenic. Phar Lap, however, had something extra: a different form of arsenic found only in the hair roots. Did this mean Phar Lap had swallowed arsenic? To check, the researchers tested the hair of a pig that was known to have died from ingesting arsenic. Their tests indicated that Phar Lap had indeed swallowed arsenic – possibly a large amount – about 35 hours before he died. What the tests couldn't show, however, was where the poison had come from.

There are many theories about how the great horse died. Which is true?

Catalyst revealed that the museum had just obtained an important new clue. A notebook kept by Harry Telford, Phar Lap's co-owner and trainer, along with Tommy Woodcock, listed the ingredients of a tonic given to horses in those days. It contained arsenic! Suspicion fell on Tommy Woodcock, who was accused of accidentally overdosing the horse. But rather than solving the mystery, yet another new finding only made it deeper. In 2011, a newspaper article from 1936 was unearthed in which Woodcock denied giving Phar Lap tonics at all. The horse didn't like tonics, so Woodcock would only pretend to administer them in order to please Harry Telford. Woodcock said he actually tipped them down the drain!

Which brings us back to square one. Where did the arsenic come from? Could it have come from the insecticide after all? Or the mafia? Had someone else given the horse the arsenic-laden tonics? Perhaps this is a puzzle that science cannot solve.

The solution to a broken heart

There's another mystery tied to the racing legend that has, fortunately, been solved. Phar Lap's heart has been on display in the National Museum of Australia in Canberra since it opened in 2001. But it's always had a slice missing!

Pieces were removed from the heart when it was tested shortly after Phar Lap died. But until recently, what happened to those pieces has been a mystery. In 2014, National Museum conservator Natalie Ison was sorting through a jar of horse parts. She was trying to decide what to include in an exhibition about horses in Australian history. Ison looked at the bottom of the jar. To her amazement, she found a label with the partly obscured word 'Lap'.

It wasn't possible to perform a DNA test on the pieces to determine if they were indeed part of Phar Lap's heart. This is because formaldehyde (the chemical used to preserve tissue samples) destroys DNA. An anatomy expert, however, confirmed the pieces fit Phar Lap's heart neatly — rather like a 3D jigsaw puzzle!

THE MYSTERIOUS MARREE MAN

A drawing of a man more than four kilometres long was found near the remote South Australian town of Marree. Who could have created this massive picture, and why has it caused such controversy?

A gigantic geoglyph

A geoglyph is an extremely large drawing etched into the ground. Geoglyphs are made by carving into the landscape through turf, soil, rock or chalk. Because they are so big, they can only be properly seen and understood from a distance.

There are several famous geoglyphs throughout the world, including England's Long Man of Wilmington, the Atacama Giant in Chile, and a monstrously huge spider that is one of the set of Nazca Lines in Peru. These all date back several centuries, offering an insight into each nation's cultural heritage.

Such drawings were not thought to exist in Australia until June 1998. That was when a pilot flying between Marree and Coober Pedy happened to spot the gigantic figure of a man carved into the plateau. The geoglyph was found just outside the Woomera Prohibited Area, the Department of Defence's weapon testing range. Not surprisingly, the discovery aroused a lot of media excitement. Could it be centuries old, like the ones in other parts of the world?

When the geoglyph was first discovered, there was only one track entering and exiting the site. Any prints or tracks that may have existed were long gone – either washed away by rain or blown away by the wind. At the time of discovery, the figure's lines were carved 20 to 30 centimetres deep. It has eroded considerably since then. This suggests the figure isn't particularly old – if it were, it would have eroded even more, perhaps disappearing completely. Besides, if it were very old, it would surely have been spotted sooner!

The design had been made by scraping off vegetation, exposing the red soil below and digging into it. Could it have been made by a plough or a bulldozer? Getting the design right wouldn't be too hard if the creator had some basic surveying skills, especially if they used a hand-held GPS (global positioning system) device. But who created it and why? Nobody has come forward to claim credit for the drawing, although that hasn't stopped speculation . . .

The American connection

According to an article published on the Living Moon website, not long after Marree Man was discovered, the media received several press releases describing the creation of the geoglyph. The authors of the press releases were anonymous. The only hint we have as to their identity is that they may have been American.

That's because the writer or writers spoke of miles and yards rather than kilometres and metres. (Most Australians, except for some older people, use the metric system.) The writer also used phrases that weren't quite right, such as the Queensland Barrier Reef, rather than the Great Barrier Reef. Mention was also made of the Great Serpent in Ohio, a prehistoric site in America that isn't well known to Australians. A sealed jar was also reportedly found near the site in a small pit. It was said to contain an American flag as well as a satellite photo of the Marree Man.

It's possible this was all done deliberately to mislead people as to the nationality of the writer. But why would anyone bother? It sounds like things couldn't get any weirder . . . But they did!

In 1999, officials reportedly received an anonymous fax from a hotel in Oxford, England, which disclosed that a plaque was buried near the figure. What the sender had to do with the geoglyph is unknown; nor is it known why they chose to send their message from the hotel. The fax said that the buried plaque was meant to have been dug up by an unnamed American media figure shortly before the Sydney 2000 Olympics. Strangely, it seems that the fax wasn't a hoax; the plaque did indeed exist! It depicted the American flag as well as the Olympic rings. Was the whole thing a big (not to mention odd) publicity stunt for the upcoming games? If so, whose idea was it? Was it the people who had sent the fax?

Interestingly, the plaque also contained a quote. It came from a book by HH Finlayson called *The Red Centre: Man and Beast in the Heart of Australia*. Published in 1935, the book dealt with natural history and anthropology (the study of human civilisations). The quote came from a section describing the hunting of wallabies with hunting sticks. Which appears to be what the figure is doing!

Is it the real deal?

Anthropologists have been arguing over whether Marree Man is an accurate drawing of a local Indigenous man. If it is, this might suggest Marree Man was created either by Indigenous people themselves or by people with expert knowledge of Indigenous culture. An article written by Penelope Debelle and published in *The Age* newspaper described the different sides to the argument.

Dr Philip Jones, an anthropologist for the South Australian Museum, insisted the image isn't an accurate representation of an Indigenous man from the area. The headdress and beard were of the wrong style, and the boomerang didn't look right. He claimed that it looked like a mashup of two different pictures that had been published in a journal. The body of one man had been mixed with the head of another – he had the photos to prove it!

However, another anthropologist claimed the figure was actually holding a throwing stick, not a boomerang. The position of the non-throwing hand was declared to be exactly right, as were the initiation scars shown on the figure's chest. Could this suggest that the Maree Man was made by someone from the local Indigenous population? If so, why has no one come forward?

Was the geoglyph etched in the ground centuries ago, or is it a modern creation?

The Marree Man geoglyph, as seen in this satellite image, appears to be of an Indigenous man holding a throwing stick.

The answer may never be known for sure, but there are some more clues as to who could have done it. *The Advertiser* newspaper published an article in 2006 suggesting South Australian artist Bardius Goldberg was responsible. He'd bragged to friends that he'd been paid $10,000 by a businessman to create a sculpture near Marree. He was familiar with GPS technology and had access to earth-moving equipment. Goldberg never admitted to being the creator, but he didn't deny it either.

What can we read into this? Did the artist have reasons for not wanting it known that he created the image? Or did he have nothing to do with it, and the real explanation for the geoglyph is something far more mysterious?

Pros and cons

The Marree Man received such interest that people were rushing to book tourist flights to view the geoglyph. This made quite a bit of money for tour operators and supporting businesses. Some Indigenous people were upset by this. A representative of the Dieri Mitha people said that the etching made a joke of their Dreaming and was exploiting her people. In other words, people were profiting financially at the expense of Indigenous cultural beliefs. She said that whoever put it there didn't understand what they were doing, suggesting she didn't think the geoglyph had been created by Indigenous people. She wanted the geoglyph removed and flights overhead banned. She expressed a hope that the person who created it would be charged by the police. The environment minister of the time agreed, calling it vandalism.

The figure remained, however, and the flights continued, until Marree Man started to fade due to erosion. Wind and rain gradually blur the edges of the lines, making it harder to see.

But is it possible that the geoglyph could actually help, rather than harm, the Indigenous people of the area? The traditional owners of the land the Marree Man is on are the Arabana people. In recent years, they've become interested in preserving the drawing. They've expressed hope it might increase the number of visitors to the area. The other local attraction is nearby Lake Eyre (or Kati Thanda). There are times when the lake is empty, which causes visitor numbers to drop. Having a second tourist attraction can help bring much-needed money into the area at those times.

THE GOSFORD GLYPHS

Mysterious carvings discovered on a rock platform near Gosford look remarkably like Egyptian hieroglyphics. Is it possible that ancient Egyptians landed on Australian shores thousands of years ago?

Walk like an Egyptian

Ancient Egyptian hieroglyphics are the last thing you'd expect to find in the Australian bush. But a chance discovery showed we should always expect the unexpected! Not many people had heard of Kariong, a leafy area near Gosford, New South Wales. Not until the startling discovery of a rock platform teeming with hieroglyphics captured the public's imagination.

Called the Gosford Glyphs, the carvings are inscribed on high vertical sandstone walls. Many of them do indeed look like genuine hieroglyphics. But how did they get there – and when?

This question was considered in the book *Encyclopedia of Dubious Archaeology*. Author Kenneth Feder, a professor of

The Gosford Glyphs are interpreted by some people as evidence that ancient Egyptians landed in Australia thousands of years ago.

archaeology, explained how the glyphs were first discovered. In 1975, council surveyor Alan Dash came across the glyphs while working. He saw a man emerge from a hole in a rock and walk away. Curious, Dash went to have a look. He found that one wall in a narrow rock corridor was covered with ancient-Egyptian-looking carvings. The other wall was bare. Over the following years he returned to the site several times, noticing that more carvings were being added all the time.

If what Dash says is correct – and there's no reason to think he would be lying – it means that the glyphs aren't very old at all. In fact, this opinion has been confirmed by geologists who noted that sandstone, which is soft, erodes quickly. If the glyphs had been made by ancient Egyptians thousands of years ago, we wouldn't be able to see them anymore. In fact, the glyphs look much fresher than nearby Indigenous rock carvings, called petroglyphs, which are known to be 250 years old.

How did they get there?

Nobody knows for sure, but there are several theories about how the carvings got there. Associate Professor Boyo Ockinga, an Egyptologist from Macquarie University, speculated that the carvings might have been made in the 1920s. Interest in

Egyptology was widespread following the discovery of Tutankhamun's tomb. Soldiers who'd been stationed in Egypt during World War I had returned home and some had been known to create similar carvings elsewhere.

Other people think the glyphs aren't even as old as the 1920s, and might have been created as late as the 1960s or 1970s. Perhaps by playful university students who were studying Egyptology and had learnt how to read and create hieroglyphics. Others talk of a mysterious man who was caught red-handed with a chisel and had his tools confiscated.

But there are people who are convinced that the carvings are thousands of years old, and were created by the ancient Egyptians themselves.

Could they be genuine?

The general view among professional archaeologists is that the glyphs aren't the real deal. They're too messy, for a start. A real Egyptian scribe would have been much neater.

In his book, Feder recounted the views of Professor Naguib Kanawati, head of Macquarie University's Egyptology department. Some of the glyphs were drawn backwards, casting doubt on their authenticity. The symbols also came from different periods of Egyptian history. In other words, symbols from eras that were thousands of years apart were grouped together haphazardly. Perhaps the biggest giveaway was the fact that some of the carvings weren't real hieroglyphics at all. One looked like a bone. Others looked suspiciously like UFOs – which ties back to the belief some people have that aliens helped ancient Egyptians build the pyramids.

Not everyone agrees with the view that the glyphs are fakes. Dr Hans-Dieter von Senff is an amateur

archaeologist (his area of expertise is in an unrelated field) and believes the glyphs are genuine. He is convinced that Australia was visited by Egyptians about 5000 years ago. But were their sailing vessels capable of making the journey? He relies on the fact that some of the engravings have been translated. They tell a story of two Egyptian princes, one of whom was bitten by a snake and died. Von Senff claims that the translation has been accepted as correct by the general director of the Cairo Museum. But even if the translation is right, does it mean an ancient Egyptian wrote the glyphs? Could the symbols simply have been copied from a book or article that told the same story? In any case, only some of the symbols told this story – the rest were unrelated or meaningless. Von Senff suggests that this inconsistency could mean the carvings were produced by an inexperienced scribe.

The belief that the glyphs are genuine was supported by Steven Strong, an amateur researcher with a passionate interest in the site. He even had an explanation for the glyphs that have been carved back-to-front, whose secret meaning he said was revealed in the ancient Egyptian Book of Thoth. Strong also maintained that local Indigenous stories supported his views that Egyptians had landed there thousands of years ago

But Strong has gone much, much further. He has co-written several books that claim he has discovered a hidden history – a revolutionary history that the academic world currently refuses to accept. Palaeontologists generally believe that homo sapiens – modern man – evolved out of Africa. Strong believes that the First Australians are separate to Africans and were really the first homo sapiens to evolve. Who knows? Although radical now, maybe his beliefs will be proved right one day!

First contact

Who were the first non-Indigenous people to make contact with the ancestors of today's Indigenous Australians? We've heard of the British arriving in 1770 and, before them, the Dutch. If the Gosford Glyphs are genuine, the ancient Egyptians may well have been the first. If the glyphs aren't genuine, then who else might have been the first to find Terra Australis Incognita, the unknown land of the south?

It might have been the Chinese, way back before America was discovered. As long ago as the early 15th century, the Chinese had a trading post in the nearby Indonesian islands. It's feasible they went to Australia, too. If they weren't the first visitors, many researchers believe it would have been the Macassans. These fishermen made annual visits from what is now Indonesia in search of sea cucumbers, which were considered a delicacy. There is evidence that they were travelling here in the 18th century, but the trips could have started much earlier.

Or could the first visitors have been East Africans? You might not have heard this theory before, but there's a good reason why it could be true. Read on and see why ...

ANCIENT AFRICAN COINS

Medieval coins from East Africa were found on a remote Australian island, far off the Northern Territory's coastline. How did they get there – and do they mean we need to rewrite our early history?

On a lonely beach, defending the nation

It might sound like a scene from a movie, but this really happened! During World War II, a young serviceman was walking along a desolate beach far from home. He felt something small and hard underfoot. Glancing down, he noticed some odd-looking coins. He scooped them up, put them in a tobacco tin, and brought them home. It was such a simple series of events, yet it sparked an investigation that may well change the way we view our country's distant past.

The windswept beach in question was on Marchinbar Island, part of the Wessel Islands group off the coast of Arnhem Land.

Who brought the ancient African coins to Australian shores – and when?

A radar unit had been set up there following the Japanese bombing of Darwin, amid fears that Australia might be invaded. The serviceman was Morry Isenberg, who worked as a radar operator for the RAAF (Royal Australian Air Force).

Isenberg found nine coins in total and had them valued when he returned home. Told they were worthless, he was filled with disappointment. Isenberg put them away for decades before finally donating them to a museum. They are now kept in Sydney's Powerhouse Museum.

Four of the nine coins turned out to be 17th- and 18th-century Dutch coins. Interesting, but not exactly earth-shattering. After all, similar coins had previously been found in Australia, and we know that the Dutch navigator Willem Janszoon made it to Australia in 1606 and that other Dutchmen followed. As for the other five coins . . . Well, that's where things get exciting.

Unlike the Gosford Glyphs (see page 258), there has been no challenge to the authenticity of the coins: they're definitely genuine. Around 900 years old, the East African coins came from the Kilwa Sultanate, based on an island just offshore from modern day Tanzania. Such coins have only ever been found outside of East Africa in Zimbabwe and Oman, relatively close to home. So how did five of these coins end up on a remote Australian island?

How did the coins get here?

These coins are the oldest non-Indigenous artefacts ever found in Australia. They raise important questions. Could their discovery mean that Africans, rather than Europeans or Asians, were the first non-Indigenous people to visit Australia?

The Wessel Islands have long been populated by the Yolngu people. Some researchers speculate that 12th-century Kilwan sailors might have used the coins to pay the Yolngu for food and fresh water before continuing on their journey. If so, then Australia might have been part of an extensive medieval trading route that linked Africa and Asia – making us less isolated than we thought.

Another theory is that the coins were brought here by the Portuguese in the 16th century. Portugal ruled Kilwa for a time, and some people believe that the Portuguese (not the Dutch) were the first Europeans to sight Australia.

The problem is that nobody knows whether the African and Dutch coins arrived on Marchinbar Island at the same time. Not knowing this makes it difficult to speculate where the two sets of coins came from. If the Dutch and East African coins had arrived at the same time, chances are that neither set was brought here by Kilwan *or* Portuguese sailors but rather they were washed onto the shore following a shipwreck. Alternatively, if the coins did arrive hundreds of years apart and just happened to have been washed onto the shore next

The coins date back over 900 years to the African Sultanate of Kilwa.

to each other around the same time, it's conceivable that the Kilwan or Portuguese sailors may have brought the East African coins. More information is needed before any firm conclusions can be drawn.

An exciting expedition

Australian anthropologist Dr Ian McIntosh had worked for many years with the Yolngu people and was up for the challenge of looking for more evidence of how the coins got there. Along with a team of archaeologists and heritage experts, he travelled to the Wessel Islands in 2013 to explore the place where the coins were found.

Mike Owen was part of the expedition, which he described in an article published in *Australian Geographic* magazine. The journey was no easy feat. Marchinbar Island is not merely remote, its terrain is very harsh. Cyclones whip through the area regularly, stirring up the sand where the coins had been unearthed so many years ago. Understandably, the researchers didn't particularly expect to find more coins – although that would of course have pleased them greatly! Rather, they were trying to find additional evidence of non-Indigenous visitors to the island to guide their investigations, such as bits of wreckage or other artefacts. An entire shipwreck would have been nice . . .

The expedition members started with a map drawn by Morry Isenberg. The serviceman had created it more than 30 years after his discovery. A failing memory may have made the map less reliable than desired, but it was all the crew had to go on. Using metal detectors, the researchers combed the island for artefacts. They uncovered many things connected with the World War II sites: bullets, rifle cartridges, burst ammunition cases. They also found a polished stone axe head, which may have indicated trade between the Macassans and the Yolngu people. They didn't find any important coins, unfortunately. Neither did they find a shipwreck. They did, however, discover a piece of timber thought to be part of an old sailing ship, which could support the European shipwreck theory.

One of the most interesting finds was the Yolngu rock art. As well as pictures of whales and fish, they found pictures of men with hats, trousers and guns – in other words, Europeans. They even found a picture of what seems to be a European steamship with a rotating propeller. Such steamships only came into existence in the 18th century – long after the times of the 12th century Kilwan sailors and the 16th-to-17th century Portuguese sailors. Does this finding suggest the African coins were part of the cargo on a steamship – or does it merely indicate that more Europeans had visited the spot than previously thought?

Some of the most valuable information came from talking to the Yolngu people and hearing their passed-down tales of contact with overseas visitors. Stories of men wearing 'mirrors' could indicate the armour worn by the Portuguese. Researchers and locals worked together to identify places where contact was likely to have taken place.

Although much was learned, Dr McIntosh recognised that this trip was only the beginning. Further exploration including another expedition is needed before the puzzle of the African coins can be solved.

The First Australians

Evidence confirms that Indigenous people were the first people who inhabited this land we now call Australia. They may have come in canoes, or they may have walked over land bridges (connections between continents) that have long since disappeared under the ocean. But when did they first arrive? The general view is that they came to Australia between 40,000 and 50,000 years ago. A recent DNA study, however, suggests it may have been much earlier – up to 75,000 years ago.

Experts from the University of Western Australia and Murdoch University were part of a team that tested a century-old lock of hair that had belonged to an Indigenous man from Western Australia. This man was chosen because it was believed he had no European ancestry. His DNA was extracted and examined and the belief was confirmed. This was very important. It meant that his DNA was suitable for examining the history of Indigenous migration prior to European contact.

If indeed the first humans did evolve into being in Africa (which is the generally accepted view) the study results suggested that the ancestors of Indigenous Australians had split from the first modern humans to leave Africa between 64,000 and 75,000 years ago.

Professor Alan Cooper, director of the Australian Centre for Ancient DNA at the University of Adelaide, said this might mean that Indigenous Australians were part of an early and separate wave of migration out of Africa, far earlier than the one that led humans to Europe and Asia. The findings have been published in an article called 'An Aboriginal Australian genome reveals separate human dispersals into Asia' in the prestigious *Science* magazine. The findings support the view that Indigenous people who live in Australia today are the descendants of the original humans who occupied Australia. As such, evolutionary biologist Professor Darren Curnoe of the University of New South Wales says that they are likely to be one of the oldest continuous populations outside of Africa.

It seems that simply everything about this big, beautiful country of ours is remarkable!

WANT MORE?

For more information about these and other strange happenings, have a look at:

- Feder K, *Encyclopedia of Dubious Archaeology: From Atlantis to the Walam Olum,* Greenwood, 2010

- Kruszelnicki K, *Curious and Curiouser,* Pan Macmillan, 2010

- Osman J, *The World's Great Wonders: How They Were Made and Why,* Lonely Planet, 2014

- Owen M, 'Unravelling the mystery of Arnhem Land's Ancient African coins', *Australian Geographic,* 7 August 2014, retrieved from http://www.australiangeographic.com.au/topics/history-culture/2014/08/mystery-of-ancient-african-coins-found-in-australia

- Putt G & McCord P, *Phar Lap – The Untold Story,* BAS Publishing, 2009

- Tim the Yowie Man, *Haunted and Mysterious Australia,* New Holland, 2006

WANT EVEN MORE?

Have you devoured all the 'Want more?' suggestions, but still hunger for more? Then have a look at the following. These are the additional sources referred to throughout the book. Most are written for adults, but don't let that stop you. Some are unashamedly speculative while others are seriously sciency . . . but maybe that's what you're craving! If so, then bon appétit!

Mythical creatures
Bunyips
- Flannery T (ed), *The Life and Adventures of William Buckley*, Text Publishing Company, 2002

- Vickers-Rich P & van Tets GF, *Kadimakara: Extinct Vertebrates of Australia*, Pioneer Design Studio, 1985

Yowies
- Sykes BC, Mullis RA, et al., 'Genetic analysis of hair samples attributed to yeti, bigfoot and other anomalous primates', *Proceedings of the Royal Society B*, July 2014, available at http://rspb.royalsociety publishing.org/content/281/1789/20140161

Drop bears
- Janssen V, 'Indirect tracking of drop bears using GNSS technology', *Australian Geographer,* volume 43, issue 4, 2012, available at http://www.tandfonline.com/doi/full/10.1080/00049182.2012.731307

The Hawkesbury River monster
- Owen J, 'Loch Ness sea monster fossil a hoax, say scientists', *National Geographic News,* 29 July 2003, available at http://news.nationalgeographic.com/news/2003/07/0729_030729_lochness.html

Hoop snakes
- Schmidt KP, 'The hoop snake story, with some theories of its origin' *Natural History,* January–February 1925, available at http://www.naturalhistorymag.com/htmlsite/master.html?http://www.naturalhistorymag.com/htmlsite/editors_pick/1925_01-02_pick.html

Tasmanian Tigers
- 'Museum ditches thylacine cloning project' *ABC News Online,* 15 February 2005, available at http://web.archive.org/web/20081015173047/http:/www.abc.net.au/news/newsitems/200502/s1303501.htm

Mysterious locations
The falling stones at Mayanup
- *Spirit Stones* documentary website, including overview report *Explanations for the Falling Stones,* at http://spiritstones.com.au/

Min Min lights
- Chalker B, 'The Min Min light revealed, nature unbound?' *The Australian Ufologist Magazine,* volume 6, number 3, available at http://www.auforn.com/Bill_Chalker_8.htm

- Pettigrew J, 'The Min Min light and the *Fata Morgana*: an optical account of a mysterious Australian phenomenon', *Clinical and Experimental Optometry,* 2003: 86: 2: 109–120, available at http://www.uq.edu.au/nuq/jack/MinMinCEO.pdf

The Devil's Pool
- Transcript of *Message Stick* documentary 'Babinda Boulders and Surf Dreaming' episode, broadcast 27 May 2005, available at http://www.abc.net.au/tv/messagestick/stories/s1381165.htm

Lasseter's Reef
- *Lasseter's Bones* documentary website, at http://www.lassetersbones.com.au/

Haunted places

Princess Theatre
- Transcript of *Rewind* documentary 'The theatre ghost' episode, broadcast 29 August 2004

Duntroon House
- Agland M, 'Sophia Susanna Campbell – Duntroon, Canberra' posted by Hidden Canberra on 26 May 2009, available at http://hiddencanberra.webs.com/apps/blog/show/1071087-sophia-susanna-campbell-duntroon-canberra

UFO sightings

The Sea Fury incident
- The J Allen Hynek Center for UFO Studies (CUFOS) website: http://www.cufos.org/

The Westall High School sighting
- *Westall '66: A Suburban UFO Mystery* website of documentary http://www.westall66ufo.com.au/westall66ufo/

The Valentich disappearance
- The transcript of the conversation between Frederick Valentich and air traffic control can be found at the UFO casebook website at http://www.ufocasebook.com/australianpilot.html
- National Aviation Reporting Center on Anomalous Phenomena (NARCAP) website at http://www.narcap.org/

Encounter on the Nullarbor Plain

- Hynek JA, *The UFO Experience: A Scientific Inquiry,* De Capo Press, 1972

- Mendham T, 'The Nullarbor UFO', *The Second Coming: All the Best From the Skeptic 1986–1990, UFOs Edition,* available at http://www.skeptics. com.au/wp-content/uploads/magazine/The%20Second%20Coming% 20-%201986%20to%201990%20collection%20-%20UFOs.pdf

The Kelly Cahill abduction

- Loftus E, 'Creating false memories', *Scientific American*, September 1997, available at https://webfiles.uci.edu/eloftus/Loftus_Scientific American_Good97.pdf

Bizarre disappearances

The loss of Ludwig Leichhardt

- Lagan B, 'What really happened to Ludwig Leichhardt?' *The Guardian,* 31 May 2013, available at: http://www.theguardian.com/ science/2013/may/31/what-really-happened-ludwig-leichhardt

Prime minister Harold Holt

- Grey A, *The Prime Minister was a Spy,* Littlehampton Book Services, 1983

- Website of Gary Simmons, who claims Harold Holt was murdered: http://www.harold-holt.net/

Baby Azaria Chamberlain

- Lindy Chamberlain's website: http://lindychamberlain.com/

The SS *Waratah*

- The Weird Australia website, which lists other ships named *Waratah* that have disappeared: http://weirdaustralia.com/2012/01/05/s-s-waratah-lost-without-trace-a-cursed-name-prophetic-dream-ghostly-omen/

The *High Aim 6*

- Bonner R, 'A fishing boat falls prey to mutiny? Pirates?' *The New York Times,* 18 January 2003, available at http://www.nytimes.com/ 2003/01/18/world/a-fishing-boat-falls-prey-to-mutiny-pirates.html

Malaysia Airlines Flight 370

- 'Missing Malaysia plane MH370: what we know', BBC News Asia online, at http://www.bbc.com/news/world-asia-26503141

Strange happenings

The human torch

- Arnold L, *Ablaze! The mysterious fires of spontaneous human combustion*, M Evans and Company, 1995

The death of Phar Lap

- Clip from ABC documentary show *Catalyst*, forensics special, available at http://www.abc.net.au/catalyst/forensics/

The mysterious Marree Man

- 'Geoglyphs of Earth', available at http://thelivingmoon.com/43ancients/ 02files/Geoglyphs_Marree_Man.html

- Debelle P, 'The evidence suggests Marree Man was created by people with expert knowledge of Aborigines', *The Age*, 26 February 2006, available at http://web.archive.org/web/20060226221348/http:/www. geocities.com/curiosities3/evidence.htm

The Gosford Glyphs

- ABC news, 'Egyptologist debunks new claims about "Gosford Glyphs"', 14 December 2012, available at http://www.abc.net.au/ news/2012-12-14/glyphs-reax/4428134

- Steven Strong's website regarding his theory of human origins: http://forgottenorigin.com/

Ancient African coins

- 'DNA confirms Aboriginal culture one of earth's oldest', *Australian Geographic*, 23 September 2011, available at http://www.australian geographic.com.au/news/2011/09/dna-confirms-aboriginal- culture-one-of-earths-oldest/

- Rasmussen M, Guo X, et al., 'An Aboriginal Australian genome reveals separate human dispersals into Asia', *Science*, 22 September 2011, available at http://science.sciencemag.org/content/early/2011/09/21/ science.1211177

GLOSSARY

artefacts human-made objects that help historians and archaeologists understand the past

ball lightning a rare form of lightning that moves in the shape of a small glowing sphere

black box equipment on board aeroplanes that helps investigators determine the cause of accidents

bunyip a mythical swamp monster

coroner a magistrate that investigates deaths to determine their causes

crop circle a very large circular shape imprinted into a field

cryptid an animal whose existence is not widely accepted by zoologists

cryptozoology the study of animals whose existence is disputed

drop bears koala-like carnivorous animals, existing only in the Australian sense of humour

geoglyph an extremely large drawing etched into the ground and visible from a distance

gullibility believing everything you are told without questioning it

Hawkesbury River monster a giant aquatic monster thought to inhabit the Hawkesbury River, whose existence is disputed

hoop snake a mythical snake that is said to be able to roll around like a wheel

megafauna large-bodied animals of a particular time or place

Min Min lights mysterious moving lights

objective impartial, or not influenced by emotions or opinions

paranormal events that are beyond the understanding of science

phenomenon an unusual or remarkable occurrence

phrenology an old belief, no longer considered valid, that a person's personality could be worked out by studying the shape of their head and their facial features

poltergeist a 'noisy ghost' or spirit that can make loud noises and cause objects to float

primary evidence an original, unaltered source of information created at the time the event occurred (such as a photograph)

pseudoscience a type of study that looks scientific but doesn't use proper scientific techniques

psychic a person who purports to have supernatural abilities, for instance being able to read minds or communicate with the dead

sceptic a person who doesn't accept things at face value and questions them

spontaneous human combustion suddenly bursting into flames for no obvious reason

subjective influenced by emotions or opinions

supernatural something that can't currently be explained by logic or science

telekinesis the ability to move objects using only the power of the mind

thylacine also called the Tasmanian Tiger, an Australian carnivorous marsupial thought to be extinct

UAP unidentified aerial phenomena; unusual lights or objects encountered by aviation professionals such as pilots while flying

UFO unidentified flying object – not necessarily alien!

ufologist someone who studies reports and evidence relating to UFOs

yowie the Australian version of bigfoot and yetis, or giant wild men, whose existence has not been proven

zoology the scientific study of animals, including their diet, habitat, and evolution

IMAGE CREDITS

p13 Illustration of the Skull found on the Lower Murrumbidgee in 1846. Reproduced from Ronald C. Gunn's 'On the Bunyip of Australia Felix' Tasmanian Journal of Natural Science, Vol. 3, No. 2, Plate 3, 1849. Courtesy of the National Library of Australia [NK3127]; p15 A Description of a wonderful large wild man, or monstrous giant, brought from Botany-Bay. Image courtesy of Mitchell Library, State Library of New South Wales [SV/44]; p22 Drop Bear © Richard Morden; p31 Plesiosaur, ichthyosaur and shark © Mengzhang | Dreamstime.com; p36 Raymond Ditmars (1876–1942). Date and photographer unknown, believed public domain and sourced from Wikimedia Commons https:/commons.wikimedia.org/wiki/File:Ditmars_Raymond_1876-1942.png; p39 National Archives of Australia: Department of Foreign Affairs and Trade; A1200, Photographic negatives and prints, single number series with 'L' [Library] prefix, 1911–1971; L35618, Fauna – Animals – This photograph of a Tasmanian Wolf or Tiger (thylacine) in captivity was taken in Hobart Zoo about 1933 and is one of the few in existence showing the animal alive, 1933; p49 Remarkable tessellated pavement at the northern end of Pirates Bay on Tasmania's Tasman Peninsula © Ekaterina Kamenetsky | Shutterstock; p60 Min Min sign in Boulia, outback Queensland, Australia. Image supplied by Tourism & Events Queensland; p65 Joan Lindsay c. 1925. Image courtesy of the State Library of Victoria Collections, www.slv.vic.gov.au; p69 Babinda Boulders, Devil's Pool Walk © Campbell Clarke; p76 Camel team in track for Lasseter's body lead by R. Buck. Image courtesy of Mitchell Library, State Library of New South Wales [a1808012];